Joseph Melling has enjoyed and maintained strong family and personal connections with the north of England and Scotland. He spent most of his working life as a professional historian, teaching in universities. His main interests are creative writing, travelling and dancing. His son Ross lives in Scotland, the setting for several stories.

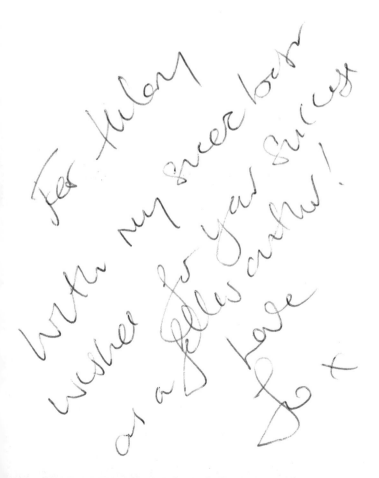

In memory of my parents, Joseph and Mary Melling.

Joseph Melling

GHOSTLY VISIONS

AUSTIN MACAULEY PUBLISHERS™

LONDON · CAMBRIDGE · NEW YORK · SHARJAH

A CIP catalogue record for this title is available from the British Library.

ISBN 9781398418493 (Paperback)
ISBN 9781398432611 (Hardback)
ISBN 9781528905022 (ePub e-book)

www.austinmacauley.com

First Published 2022
Austin Macauley Publishers Ltd®
1 Canada Square
Canary Wharf
London
E14 5AA

These stories were written in 2020–21. Many were presented to the Short Story Writing Group of Bristol and Bath Meetup, which I formed with others in 2021. I benefitted from the comments and suggestions, as well as the companionship, of group members and wish to record my appreciation of their creative criticism and encouragement.

Table of Contents

Preface

The collection of mainly very short stories presented here were written recently, among a larger group of stories addressing similar themes. The main thread in these stories is that of strange and unexpected visitations, many with some supernatural thread or concern, though others deal with 'visions' in a broader sense. There are thirty-five stories of approximately 1000 words each, designed to be read easily, some mainly consisting of dialogue but most are first-person narratives. Each of the stories is designed to be compact but with scope for expansion to greater length without compromising the succinct nature of the tales. These thirty-five are selected from a larger number of stories I have written in the past year or two and more stories as well as longer versions of these stories can be provided.

Varying in subject and context, the thread holding the stories together remains that of visits or visitations which change the lives of the characters, often fundamentally. Most are situated in Britain, though they range in time from the prehistoric past to an uncertain time in the future when very different rules for civilisation and survival exist. In some of the 'exotic' stories there is a clear accent of Argentine and South American interest in a few of them. Though the time horizon of the stories vary, the historical setting should be both clear and accessible to the reader. The sections indicate the broad direction of different stories within the theme of visions and visitations. The sections on 'unexpected reunions' includes often exude a sense of menace or suppressed violence and the intention throughout is to hold the reader in some suspense until the outcome offers different kinds of resolution.

Section 1:
Unearthly Visions

The Visitor

Jean avoided looking at the empty page which lay on her writing desk and she lit her cigarette. She stared out, unseeing, at the blank, black fields that lay around her shack and wondered when the day would come. If light stole across these benighted hedges, then she might remain unvisited.

Watching the tip of her *gauloise* burning in the gloom of the cottage, her mind drifted back to those first cigarettes. Smoked in Paris in the 1920s when she still believed in youth and fame. Her married lover usually left after midnight and she was able to write and reflect on time passing in the city of pretended romance. She reflected without bitterness how French men had made love to themselves while the women luxuriated in the illusion of love. They each tried to give sexuality without feelings some significance. If you can't do it, then talk about it or better still write about it. Was she any better with her novels of sex without shame in the life of the 'modern woman'? Stylish only as long as you have glamour. After that you're a whore to yourself.

Jean's reverie was interrupted by the gong of the clock and she halted all thought to await the moment. She heard her visitor answer the clock with her strange high-pitched laugh. Refusing to turn her head towards the shadow she finally broke the silence, hearing herself echo that eerie call of hysterical joy that had announced the arrival.

"I knew you would return. You insist there be no fear, no screaming fits for you. You only ever screamed when he entered your private attic. But those final moments on the battlements of that forbidding fortress? Did you call for him from that dark tower, a damsel enticing her fatal lover as the flames caressed you both?"

Jean realised she was only delaying the inevitable. Indulging herself when she knew her work awaited. Reluctantly but with purpose she rose and slid into her writing chair and reached for the fountain pen she had possessed most of her life. One of the few gifts he had given her that she had not sold or otherwise surrendered to the pawnbroker. Jean saw the shadow move across her desk but ignored the distraction.

"I have one or two questions, Antoinette. You hold him responsible for carrying you off from Caribbean sunshine, tethering you to a cold, dark Moorland life. You were never a Rochester (or even a Bronte), I grant you that. Never asked to haunt the wild wastes of an ugly, unfamiliar country. Tropical souls like you and I die among the wintry indifference of the English. But why not stay out there in the sun with all its diabetic decadence?"

Jean waited and understood. "Well, as you say, he was never handsome but he was different. He had all that manly vigour that promised endless children and a line of obedient servants. Those over-familiar cheats that served us in the sunshine could be discarded forever."

Jean felt her visitor's interest fading and moved to hold the stream that trickled away from her. She concentrated on the memory of the *obeja* she had met as a girl, pressing her fingers to her choker for some solace. The visitor remained. Jean renewed her interview.

"Believe me, I know the outrage of being misunderstood, misrepresented. I know that rage. Granted, you never accepted that name." A plain rasping sound of breathless exasperation. "Bertha!" Anyone flushed with the fragrance of Martinique bouquets would have refused such a vulgar re-Christening. But tell me: were you ever a Mason? Being fathered or mothered, elsewhere and arriving on the wrong side of the sheet? It would at least exculpate your brother's incestuous obsessions."

The presence said nothing, expressed no fury at this interrogation. Jean continued to write, "I am taking down your statement as clearly as I can, Antoinette, but you must help me. You say you intended to murder Jane but struck on the plan of destroying your husband as a way of ruining her life. Was she then a worthy opponent? A little nobody with those paltry English breasts, reaching for the Bible to prop up her ridiculous reasoning."

The room darkened. Jean realised she had made a crass mistake of some kind. The clock struck again. She knocked over the ash tray and heard it smash on the linoleum. "Yes, I see now, your real murderer is Charlotte. I see that. Making heroines out of plain Janes, beatifying them as patron saints, protectors of crushed little governesses, searching for the sensual grope of fate in their bookish meetings while preserving their feminist puritanism like a decayed wedding cake. Yearning for but terrified of a good fuck, for fuck's sake. Timid lesbian flirtations but pulling back from the real thing."

Jean recalled her lesbian flings in forgotten Parisian clubs before the Germans stamped their twisted version of homosexual outrage on our memories. Pondering her past, she felt anger rising.

"Why now?" she demanded. The shadow was unmoved.

"Well, it's too bloody late! I don't want your sodding revelations, your inspired little confessions. Francophile charm won't work on me. I've had enough squalid duplicity – men and women – to last more than a lifetime."

But Jean had spent most of her life adrift on that strange Sargasso Sea called rural England. Devon if you like. Desiring literary fame more than any penis she had ever held or swallowed, it had been denied her. And now it was offered. Too late. The only thing to do was publish and tolerate the unwanted adulation that would urinate over her like a broken drainpipe.

At last, she turned to face the shadow and saw the familiar bottles of untouched medication. Her brother had threatened a return to the hospital if she made another 'episode' in the bloody village. Sod him. She'd burn down this mad woman's attic first. As morning broke across the untrodden landscape, she lit a final cigarette.

Holy Skin: A Crusade

The blue tube flickering in the window, showered light on tattered photographs of faces and limbs which were inked in intricate ways. The epileptic effect bestowed by the light increased the sense of entering an unreal domain. An impersonal place for intimate encounters between a tattooist's needle and willing flesh. A pink neon sign outside the massage parlour next door offered an alternative guiding light to the uncertain clientele. Facing them, the gates of a darkened cemetery completed the scene. Long faded from its heavy Victorian grandeur, the cemetery was still capable of exerting its presence on this once-affluent area of the sprawling city.

The man with the greying beard crouched over the arm of a familiar customer. His client's thick fore-limbs were saturated with images and symbols that marked out convictions and caprices, down to his hardened knuckles. Ringed and clasped with metal from fingers to wrists, he smoked a self-rolled cigarette as he stared vacantly toward the window. The needle man ignored everything but the point of injection, confident that the pain would not trouble this client. He worked steadily without conversation.

Neither man was expecting the half-glazed door to open and another figure to join them. The owner spoke first.

"I'll be a while on this. Did you make an appointment?"

"No. But I can wait."

"I'll be shutting in a couple of hours or so."

"I won't detain you long."

"What is it you're looking for?"

The biker interjected, "Do we have a problem?" He glanced at the arrival. The question hung between the three of them, moving in no particular direction.

"Don't think so," said the tattoo artist. "He can wait."

The entrant sat near the door and picked up a magazine featuring motorcycles and young women on its cover. The tattooist returned to work as the biker drew a final drag on a shrivelled cigarette and dropped its remains on the scarred linoleum floor.

The only sound drifting through the room was the buzzing of the needle. Occasional cars slid by in the darkness or slowed to a crawl outside the massage parlour. Almost an hour passed and the biker rose heavily from the chair, blowing on his fresh insignia.

"I like it."

"Well, we didn't have a lot of space so I had to work it in against the serpent's head. Are you heading next door?"

The biker nodded and pushed a fold of banknotes forward. The owner nodded without counting it as his customer pulled on a leather jacket. His progress to the door was abruptly halted when his leathered arm was seized by the stranger. The biker's face darkened in fury and then relaxed into stillness as the stranger moved to hold his left hand. When he released it, the biker awoke as from a trance and without looking at either man, moved out of the shop.

The owner stared at the man sitting in the chair.

"You know him?"

The stranger answered in a leisurely tone, "In a roundabout way."

"What is it I can do for you?"

"Give me an opinion."

"On what? I do tattoos, not opinions."

"They're the same thing." He dropped his long coat on the seat and opened a black shirt. The tattooist stared at a torso covered almost black with a menagerie of creatures that occupied the thin body. Only a shoulder retained a pale pallor.

"You didn't get those done around here. Don't recognise the work."

"No. Mostly done in Riga. A couple in Hamburg. One in Bucharest."

"You've travelled around then." Pausing. "What is it you want?"

"A question answered. You think you can match the quality – the feeling of this work? Can you meet them?"

"Meet them? I don't know. It would take a while. Probably two sessions."

"You have one. Tonight. The price is irrelevant."

The owner had not smoked in two years. He pulled open a stiff wooden drawer and fumbling an open pack of stale cigarettes, he lit one and considered his uninvited guest.

"What do you want?"

"The shoulder. I need the face of a boy." He drew a drawing from his open shirt pocket. A boy with open, dark eyes.

"Just that?"

"Just that but with the wings of an angel rising behind his head."

The tattooist drew in a breath of tobacco smoke and shrugged. "It'll cost—"

"I said the price was irrelevant, didn't I? Just do the boy justice." He laid an odd emphasis on the last word and moved into the chair, closing his eyes.

There was no conversation. The tattooist felt frustrated that he could summon no power to refuse the commission, though he was reluctant to have any dealings with this weird pushy stranger. He could usually turf anyone out of his shop without a second thought. It was almost eleven when he completed the last feather of wings adorning the boy's head. The client turned his shoulder in the mirror.

"Competent" was all he said. He handed the artist a tight sheaf of notes and surprisingly, returned to sit near the door.

"Anything else? I'm about to close."

"Just a few minutes." With this he turned his seat to the window facing the road.

Shortly, they saw the biker walk to a powerful motorcycle with a woman in train. He kicked the machine into action and turned in an arc around the road, heading south. As he completed the manoeuvre, his left arm felt stiffly to his side and the accelerating bike curved erratically away, crashing noisily into the cemetery gates. There he was pinned with his passenger flung back on the road.

The tattooist exclaimed, "Holy Christ!"

The man responded casually, "Not really. No help from there."

The tattooist finally found his anger. "Just who the hell are you? And this boy on your fucking arm? What is it psycho – some angel of death?"

The man put on his long coat. "No. He was killed by a biker. Just like him. Long time ago." He opened the door and walked slowly towards the cemetery gates.

Lanterns

He had been waiting for something new. Something to arrest his imagination. Teaching school had lost its excitement for Owen after fourteen years in one of the less spectacular Welsh valleys. Occasionally, a bright pupil shared his passion for poetry and the history of long dead civilisations but even bright children moved on. To greener pastures. In flight from boredom, his interests had shifted to restoring old magic lanterns which had once offered a living income for a handful of men traversing these valleys with their humble farming and odd mining villages. That was before these moving pictures had arrived. Now there were three 'picture houses' or 'cinemas' in this area alone and many more in far-off coastal towns. It was easier to find work playing an old piano in these picture theatres than to gather enough pennies to make a magic lantern show worthwhile.

The old lanterns were sold off cheaply or left to rust away in untidy back rooms. He was not against the new craze with its comic stars and silent gunfights. His neighbour thought otherwise. Mrs Ellis was adamant that these places were no better than gin palaces; they were worse because decent men and women might visit these 'dream traps', even if they had taken a temperance pledge against all drink. But the pictures could lead people astray and draw them away from the real spoken word you could hear in the chapel on Sunday morning.

So fervent was Mrs Ellis in her narrow religious purity that he was surprised to hear other neighbours tell how she had been quite famous in her younger years for 'the gift'. She had supposedly had a second sight and people came to her to ask her to explain the Lord's will in taking their children or leaving them without this or that. She was always reluctant to offer any opinions though she had patiently tried to comfort those in distress. Her husband never interfered and never questioned why they were without children. After his passing she tended their garden and helped to keep the chapel clean.

One morning she caught sight of him over their shared garden wall and seemed to stop, transfixed by his figure. Recollecting herself she nodded and smiled but went indoors. A few moments later she reappeared and stood in her gardening gloves waiting. He asked how she was and she thanked him before asking, "And how are you, Mr Phillips? Are you keeping well?" Slightly surprised, he assured her he was fighting fit. Her next comment was slightly eccentric. 'Why don't you spend more time out doors? Walking in the hills I mean. It's a lot healthier than working with dusty old relics, isn't it?"

She could only mean his hobby, which was odd as he had not told many people of his secret passion for the lanterns. He smiled in agreement. The conversation was soon forgotten as he worked with a particularly fine, brass-encased, magic lantern that he found in a junk shop on a visit to the coast. The slides included a set of prints showing a figure riding a horse across a bridge and against a sharp horizon. Another set revealed soldiers marching in rows towards a town with steeples. As he watched he saw something curious. A dark figure moved across the sky and quickly disappeared behind a steeple. Inspecting the images he could just see what looked like a Pegasus, a flying horse, skirting the tops of the roofs. It didn't seem to fit in any clear story being told but there it was.

The restoration went well and he suggested to his head teacher that he might put up a show for the children at the end of the school year, which was rapidly approaching. His superior was enthusiastic and Owen worked steadily on his equipment. The day arrived and he was carrying his lantern towards his headmaster's car for the short ride to school when he saw the curtains of Mrs Ellis's window part slightly as she gazed out. At that moment he heard the heavy crank of an auto bus as it rounded the corner and a little girl ran forward to pick up her pieces of chalk from the road. Owen had no time to think but ran forward calling her to come back. A horse drawn dray stopped before the corner as the omnibus careered forward.

The accident report relied on the testimony of the headmaster, sitting in the driver's seat of his car waiting for his colleague to load the lantern through the open door on the passenger side. The bus swerved to avoid the girl and took the car door off its hinges before hitting the horse cleanly in mid-body. With a smack the horse was thrown ten feet through the air and landed heavily on Owen, whose body was crushed against the lantern as they horse and teacher collapsed together against the edge of the pavement.

Mrs Ellis quietly closed her curtains. She did not feel up to attending chapel that Sunday.

Meeting Place

The shaving mirror looked back at him with an odd stare. *He must be getting old*, he thought as he paused with the razor to consider the day. Washing his face he descended to make morning coffee and watch the sun rise over the far hills. Tasting the slightly bitter African beans he heard a click. The fingers of the wall clock had become entwined and the minute hand was struggling to free itself. From a chair he lifted the clock and adjusted the hands. The remedy was not effective as the minute now clicked standing alone as though unwilling to advance the hour any further. Mechanical failure. Sitting again he saw that the clock on the cooker showed the same reluctance to move. Something must be affecting electric and battery power in the house. Was it atmospheric? A kind of electric storm? The house was on the lee of a hill from which you could see pylons in the near distance, marching across the landscape, tied together like blind men with outstretched arms. The reception was patchy at the best of times. The signals for cell phones were poor and the internet was liable to go awry at unexpected moments. It was time for him to think of leaving this place. What kept him here? He had no visible ties to this area though he had resisted opportunities to move when they had been offered.

As he thought about the eccentric beginning to the day, he was reassured by the steady increase in the light as he watched the hedgerow of the nearest field come to life in the morning air. The heavy branches of the oak tree were showing fresh leaves in the early spring and birds moved in upper reaches of the ancient structure. Then something unexpected came into view. A young boy wearing light clothes and a trailing scarf appeared, running along the hedge from left to right. As he came within the shadow of the tree, a branch collapsed and almost hit him. The boy must have heard the break and movement, swerving to avoid it. He paused briefly to look up at the dangerous bough and ran on out of the framed picture of the window. As he watched he wondered, 'Who was that boy? Was he local? Or was he more familiar than that?'

The unexplained drama stirred a remote memory in the watcher. Before he could explore his recollection he saw an older man striding slowly from the direction the boy had just run. What was going on? The village was a mile away and few walkers came this way. Public footpaths led across the side of the hill, not behind his house. This older man, he decided, must be connected to the child who had escaped injury. Perhaps his grandfather, coming to see the danger which had nearly claimed his grandson. As the old man gazed up at the tree, a bird rose suddenly and another branch fell. This time the branch was lighter but the man could not move so readily and the broken wood struck him, glancing off his shoulder and sending him to the ground.

He struggled to his knees and as he rose to his feet, the boy reappeared from the right. They quickly embraced as equal survivors of a powerful enemy that stood just above them. As he gazed in wonder at this spectacle, the two figures turned toward the man's window and returned his interrogating look. They were utterly calm and simply stood. Waiting. Speechless. He knew what they were recalling. That he had a very similar near-accident as a child when he was playing near his grandfather's house, not long before the affectionate old man died. Just at this time of the seasons. The morning breeze combed the grass as the three of them contemplated the near embrace of the tree.

In the kitchen the only sound was the continued clicking of the halted clock. He rose. He did not take his coat as he left by his back door to meet the waiting figures. Conscious of all the strangeness of the encounter he left without any sense of fear or even any reluctance.

Angelus

There was no one else in the house after the removal men left the last packing case in the hall. His dad had gone to the supermarket to buy them some food and his mum was in the garden talking to the new neighbour about the days when the recycling van called. Through the kitchen window he could see the long arches of the railway viaduct that stood in the distance, framing the horizon of the little town where they had come to live. He was to be given the bedroom that looked across the valley to the viaduct and when his new brother or sister arrived, they would be in the smaller bedroom next to his.

He had wanted to stay in the last house, where his school could be seen and his friends came to play in the big garden. His dad said this town was better for work and that his mum wanted to be nearer to his gran with the new baby. He didn't cry but he felt dry tears inside him when he thought about having to find his way without his friends. But he liked the bigger bedroom and he wondered if he could find the box that held his board games and best books.

Then he saw him. He didn't know what moved when he first looked. Maybe the figure had been crouching down. When he stood up, the shape was clearly that of a tall man, thin not fat, standing there. On top of the viaduct. What was he doing? Did he have on some kind of helmet? There was a slight flash of sunlight or something when he turned his head. The boy was far away and could just make out the movement so he ran upstairs to his new bedroom. When he reached the window the man was still standing and he seemed, even so far away, to be looking directly at their house. After a moment he stretched out his arms as though he was ready to fly and he leapt forward and down towards the stony stream that lay far below the arch of the viaduct.

He didn't fall like a stone but sort of flew down, like a stone bird or the angels you saw on the old gravestones that stood in the churchyard at their last town. He seemed to halt or stop for a moment and then disappeared. Maybe he crashed or he could have gone into the water but there was no water deep enough to take his fall. At least the boy didn't think so.

His mother called and he went downstairs. He didn't feel he could tell her about the man jumping and she was busy looking for bedding they could put on the bare mattresses that lay in each bedroom. When Dad came back, they used the cooker that was left by the last people to cook themselves some food. That night he looked again for the figure on the viaduct through the un-curtained window but saw only the lights of the town. Days went by and he began at the local school and met someone called David, who might be his friend. The next morning before breakfast he caught sight of the man again. So he must have survived his last jump. Somehow. There was a slight drizzle. Then something strange happened. The man waved. He was somehow certain that the man was waving to him. Was he saying hello? Or goodbye? Or just waving? Then he turned and taking the same position with his arms outstretched, he jumped. The same flight path and the same odd ending.

At school he played football with David and decided he could ask him about the viaduct. David listened and nodded. "They used to let people go up there sometimes. But they stopped."

"Why?"

"Last year a man started bungee jumping but one of his ankle ropes snapped. So he got smashed on the rocks."

The boy felt sad for the jumper and he knew it was the same one that he saw. But he was glad that he waved to him. It was to welcome him to this town. He felt the man was telling him not to be afraid. He never appeared again so he must have been happy with his last jump. At least for now.

Mapping Time

As a boy he loved to study antiquated maps which early adventurers had used to find their way around unexplored continents. The coastlines drawn for the first time and strange new creatures discovered in the near interior. Though he lived in an age of space travel where the moon was captured and pictured in black skies, *Treasure Island* remained his favourite book and Robinson Crusoe the hero, whose real-life prototype, Alexander Selkirk, had grown up near his grandparents' home on the eastern coast of Scotland. Like Crusoe he had a tense connection with his father and had refused all encouragement to 'get a trade' or 'find a good office job' as he went hitch-hiking in search of experiences that couldn't be found in the dark streets of his respectable northern town. Making good money from pushing out fine iron and steel was enough for young men who had their sights fixed on a nice suit or a local girl.

When he finally returned from a year in South America he understood the empty places and deep poverty that the first explorers must have seen. People who wanted to conquer new worlds had been wilfully blind to the suffering that could be found even in the most beautiful places like the slavery and intended sacrifice of Man Friday. Or they were determined to believe their own religion gave them the right to trample across virgin lands and claim possession of earth that they had never seen. Walking along deserted roads in southern Chile had revealed the real depth of insignificance that can sweep across the solitary life. The beauty of the cold seas was only disturbed by killer whales in search of unsuspecting seals. The strangest discovery he made in that desolate place, where even the Jesuit missionaries had neglected as devoid of people and purpose, was a sense of God hovering above the empty horizons. Perhaps the Buddha would have sensed the prevalence of a transcending nothingness in these places where few humans had ever settled or even wandered. Terra del Fuego had held its sparse scattering of natives, wandering naked against the fierce elements of storm and sky but this long vertebra of rock backed against the endless Pacific, had retained its brutal purity in pristine solitude, unpeopled.

If his travels had instilled a fresh consciousness of the urgent need to protect natural landscapes against irreversible damage, he was less convinced of the value of political agitation than the prospect of living the good life close to the earth. He joined a small cooperative partnership selling adventure holidays to backpackers and bored package tourists. In the slower winter months he worked with a consultancy, helping those with money or capacity to find a slower life in downsized occupations. Few of his relationships gave him the thrill he had found walking alone in uncharted paths and his dreams returned to the coastline where he might find the cottage that could hold his interest. One autumn night it appeared, out of the dusk, like a moving image. Close to the heather and bracken that tumbled down the steep sides to the sea, deserted but with a note attached to the door 'For Sale.

Private sale only'. There was a contact number answered by an elderly lady. Her brother had lived there until his death the previous spring. "It's cash only," she said but named a very low price.

As he was clearly interested she hesitated. "Maybe something further inland would suit you better." No, this was what he wanted.

"You realise you have to take it as it is? Warts and all." Yes, he understood.

"My brother was not fussy. He knew his days were numbered." He made no reply.

And so it was done. He was moved in before winter had really set in and built a good fire with dried wood. The next summer he was away and decided against renting it to holidaymakers but on returning in a rain-sodden autumn he could see some of the earth had tumbled toward the bracken. Within eighteen months the ground on which his cottage stood had receded noticeably and his home now hung at the lip of the terrain before it tumbled downwards. Even so, it could hardly be called a cliff. Slowly and with deliberation nature claimed more of his land and his gable wall first cracked and finally the supports he had fixed to protect it gave way. His cottage was steadily eroding along with the ground on which it stood. It had been happening for years, without troubling the elderly man who had remained there. No sighing of sadness could be heard in the winds that helped this movement of the earth. How could we complain? He retrieved most of the good stone left in the building and stacked it as a wall at the further end of his ground, together with the unbroken slates from the roof. The remainder he left for the sea and one day packed his camper van for the long road that swept to the skyline.

Section 2:
Long Visions

The Strangers

Before they came, we could still measure the land by throwing. We tested how far a stone could fly and how fast an arrow could rise before it fell into hard or soft earth. In those times I spent many cold days making new heads for arrows and the scrapers we used to skin the animals. My kinfolk taught me how to work both stone and make the metal we needed to survive in this land. Wild beasts killed us but it was people we feared more. We still used flint as well as hard grey stone for our walls and to grind our crops, the sharp edges of the flint catching light and shadow as does the moon. In darker days of winter we also catch fish in the deep lakes and travel to the salted sea every month to find more. Leaping fish and shell-creatures were good eating, fresh or salted.

Our memories taught us our enemies and how far they stood from us. If they took or killed anyone, we did not rest until we found them and brought the invaders back to face the families. If we could not get them here, we killed them and brought their heads. Until we were revenged, our people went to them again, making them suffer our pain.

These strangers changed the way our lives were reckoned. Our ground was shaken from hill to river. We no longer saw distances with certainty. They appeared first digging, using bright metal hooks and hammers we had never seen, splitting rocks and trees without stopping. They did not talk to the forests or the hills but simply walked together, like shadows of each other, in straight lines. They made the earth solid with a stone path for walking. One of us was caught watching and they tried to take words but learned nothing of us. They beat him with sticks and released him. We knew then they did not fear us but could make us give all we had, even our children and cattle.

They were warriors. When they made their stone ways, men stood in metal clothes with spears and swords that shone in daylight. Our settlement was not strong enough to fight them and the far hill-people would not join us. Some tried to waylay one of their soldiers but were badly beaten by the sword-carriers. Our neighbours lost some strong warriors and their chief was driven back, wounded. Then these neighbours came to us, offering antlers and one half of an elk horn if we would join with them and with their sister-fort which stood further away and was untouched by the strangers.

No decision was made. We waited. Then we saw the strangers make their wall of stone. Not only wooden stakes for their encampment along the rock road that led towards us. This wall was something we had never seen, with stones that had edges almost as straight as a spear shaft, fixed together as tightly as a skin. They made a second wall, deeply from first and earth was thrown between them. Men could stand on this rampart and watch us from afar. Some older ones in our tribe said that was as far as the strangers wanted to go. Even they knew that this was not true. The strangers would come for us and take us back to the wall, those that were not slain in the taking.

Before moving we tried to talk to our gods and find what the spirits of people who lived before wanted us to do. They told us that we must stand or we must fly, leaving all the land we knew and hide from these bright swords until we could hide no more. If we went away from the wall, then other peoples like ours might turn against us, fearing we would take their hills and hunt their wild beasts.

At this time, I spoke, though not a chief. I said we should find out more about these strangers as they were strong. Danwaith went with me to their wall without weapons. They seized us but did not hurt us, bringing us to a chief of theirs who sat. He watched us with stone-grey eyes, listening to our speech but not hearing. We think that they came from a place far away. The chief had a gold helmet and showed us a white horse on which he rode. They held many weapons in a stone house behind the wall. He gave me a gift of a piece of round metal with the face of a man on one side and an eagle on the back. It shone like a silver moon, brighter than any metal I had seen.

They laughed when they released us. We returned to our people, though my heart burned in me. For I could see from their stone and metal that the strangers were a mighty people and would not be overcome, however, brave our fighters. I yearned to learn what these newcomers had to teach and to find out how they made so many things well. It was clear that this would not happen, for my people would see their lives torn up like skins and changed in ways that would leave them mindless, no longer able to measure out the world or find the way they could be. We would be trampled like stone, cut into straight lines and made to fit into a fixed wall with soldiers standing on top of us and treading our earth down until we could breathe no more.

This is why we have to fight them and if we remain true to our gods, then perhaps after we have been slaughtered before the walls or driven along strange roads, the almighty ones will send storms and winds that will, in time, wash away their stone and send it down the rivers into the sea. Where the fish still swim and wait.

Flight

The Walls spoke to us again last night. We had waited until the Moon was full and had passed before we looked at them. Assa first told the signs after the last attack by the dark-haired ones. We lost three warriors and four wood spears in that attack. Six of them were slain – two only hurt and then put to the fire afterwards. But they attack in greater numbers every time they come. The earthen ramparts are strong and can be repaired but we now have the young ones helping to watch at night and they fall asleep unless beaten.

When Assa told us what the Walls said, we waited for Meoh, Assa's mother to come and give her words. She spent a whole night gazing at the Wall, chewing dark nuts. Meoh added to the Wall with chalk and ochre, ground with her nuts and spittle. She made hand figures on the Wall, joining what the Old Ones had made long before this time. Some say before the ramparts were made soon after our people came from the marshlands as waters rose and we left and learned to use the land up here. Up here we are nearer the Old Ones who have passed into the sky to join the moon when it called them.

When Meoh had spoken, we gathered our wise people and we are chanting together to make knowledge of where we are to go as a people. Our two elders are to chant alone after and tell us their wisdom. Only then will we know how to give word-time to what Meoh saw and what line our people may then run along to the far horizon. We will move by moonlight.

This is a turning-time for me. I knew it would come. I made four children with Neah. Three survive, two daughters and one strong son. He must race the years and become a man before his time. When they go I will hold him in my arms and give him as much strength as I can. The people must leave in two groups or they will be seen and taken. The rampart men will stay with me and we await the final attacks of the dark ones. We must repel their rage or they will overrun us and know our families have gone. Those travelling will then be hunted too soon. We must make the fight last and kill and torment as many as we can. Then we will burn and attract more. We will finish our time killing them and finding our own death with them. In this way we can know that this ground is still sacred and assure the Old Ones in the Wall that we did not abandon them but stayed to the end of this earth's time. We will end fighting with our backs against the Wall that has protected and guided us. They will witness our coming into the Wall to join them.

One day I hope to revisit these places and to gaze from the moon at the things that my people do in their new homes. Some of our people believe that we can never regrow the ground where we found shelter after the ancient time of the marshes. This is not what I believe. My belief is that all of life is going and growing.

The dark-haired ones may be sent by the enemy spirits who hate our people or they may be messengers to us that we must now find a new way. For almost all of three times a man's life we have been working to make this thing called metal. The thing that a man brought to the camp long years, countless moons ago. He said it came with a trader who crossed a wide water on a wooden raft with sails. We have now almost made things and tipped spears with some rough metal that survived the fire-making. There is little of the hard-earth we need for the metal-making in this land around us but more near the dark hills on the line of the sky we see on clear days.

We can take our cattle and animals, though we have only one strong horse. But my son will ride him one day and with a metal spear he will come back and see where his father sat and hunted with him. And he will watch the moon and I will look down and find that my time was well spent. His mother will chant and my daughters will find the wisdom of the next time for our people. This rises from a deep yearning. It is my faith in the life of our blood.

Unbroken Sky

These things that we need for our lives, these rocks that the earth gives us, the seeds that the soil cherishes, the rain that the sky gives to feed our land and our rivers. The sky, we know, is held up by the great tree of light with its great fruit the sun, falling to earth each night and re-growing before dawn. In its battles with the great cold wind, the sun is forced back into itself every year and hardly grows to warm our lands. Then we await its return, freeing our world from deadly cold and giving new life. Even in winter we see that the leaves of the tree remain alight, shining through the dark days and moving to make shapes as they regrow every year.

When branches of the great tree fall to earth, we watch the sky scored white, cut by the storm as the light cuts through the air and pierces the ground like spears. The great rolling noise is the sound of the Great Ones, clapping their hands against their legs in wrath, warning us that anyone hit by the light will die, burned like the dry grass that rages when the light is not washed away by rain and accepted by the river gods who swallow the fire sent to them by the tree.

We have so much to learn, harvesting this sacred ground. Our people have long-honoured the Sky-Tree and the earth that gives life but what do we know of things beyond this?

Things that have been and no longer are? Time is a dark horizon. It cannot be counted beyond the memories of those who know. We came to these hills long ago and settled on this hill. We can see any who come to us and we are ready to welcome or resist. Those across the river tried to take our children in the past and the river rose to protect us and to tell us that we must move to this place where we are safe for now.

Alongside our hill we see another, smoother, shaped like the back of a drinking horse or an outstretched arm pointing. We know that this was made by people's long ago, perhaps helped by the gods but we know of a door that can be entered, though we do not go in for there are dead people, who rest until they are called. Why they were placed in a great hill made by others we do not know. Perhaps their gods wanted this. But those gods have died or gone away. Our gods killed them or drove them away. For the gods who guide us drive the rivers this way or that and they fill the rivers with fish and other creatures. They made a marriage with the earth and can command things. When the strangers came and attacked us, we had to leave the riverside for this hill. But we will go back and honour our dead. When we kill and capture those who attack us, we shall throw a victorious spear and one metal sword, however, precious to us, into the waters as a gift. The gods can see we honour them in our victories.

We had no sight of how the gods live and how our gods came to be powerful. Our people had the stories of how the sky came to cradle us and how we found the way to the mountain and the making of metals that have given us our survival. But no one is alive with us who has seen the gods. No one but me. I spoke to the elders and they told me it was a dream but that I was chosen to have such dreams. It was like

47

no other dream because I was awake and walking. So I must recount what happened and perhaps tell my son how it was, so that it will not be lost.

As we set our traps for the wolves and the bears around our camp, I could see that men hunters would know how to side-step them and come for us. With two others I stayed awake and guarded the hillside. At dawn the rain came and the river rose during the day. In the evening I rested but was troubled and lay awake before rising to watch the hill again. There I saw things.

The rain passed and the land was drying. It was strange to see stalks of light, the branches of the great tree that lives beyond the sky and gives us life. But this night there was no rain and no clapping. All was silent even as the light descended and pierced the earth like spears. Anyone caught by these spears is certain to die. This night was strange for I saw a few creatures, not men but not wolves running fast across the plain beyond the hill and they were hit by the light and they shone in its brilliance but kept on running. As they were caught by the light they ran together in a round like a grinding stone and there was some way in which the light gathered the stones themselves around like a people. This was not my dream but could be seen in the morning, where stones stood together and had counsel beyond our hill.

There was no one to see but myself and I had to see if these things held out danger for our people, whether these creatures were another kind of animal or some wayfarers that come to destroy us, though they did not look like men. With my spear I ventured down to the circle.

Section 3:
Turning Points

Suspended

The man in the dark coat turned to the apprentice.

"You said Donleavy?"

"Yes, sir."

"Donleavy. Do you know what a visionary is?"

"Not really, sir."

"Guess. Speculate."

"Someone who has visions, sir? Like a prophet? Perhaps?"

"Not bad. A person who has visions. Could be a prophet. Could be Joan of Arc facing the fire. A visionary is someone like Joan, who asks you to suspend your disbelief. They leave you hanging. In suspense, if you like."

"How does one do it, sir? I mean, hang us like that?"

"You have to defy 'wisdom' – the knowledge we get handed down to us like old furniture. A visionary wants to burn old furniture, just as Joan of Arc burned."

The apprentice said nothing. The engineer walked to the edge of the cliff and looked down. He turned and pivoting again, fired another question at his young companion.

"You have heard of Christopher Wren?"

The young man hesitated. "Was he the one who rebuilt London – after that big fire?"

The engineer hardly paused. "When he showed them his plans of Saint Paul's they insisted that he should put in more pillars to hold the roof more than he needed, to keep that whole magnificent pile of heavy stone standing. What did he do? I can hear you asking…"

The apprentice said nothing.

"He didn't try to convince them – once he saw that they were ruled by fear. His own imagination, that was fearless, flew like a bird, rising – as you said – from the ashes of London. But they wanted to tether that phoenix to cage that brilliant mind. So, he didn't waste words on them. He simply put in the pillars and made sure they were an inch or two shorter than the main supports. They didn't hold up anything. Redundant, just like those rigid minds he had fought to free. Their brains seized up. Stopped like a broken clock."

"No one could stop you though, sir. Could they?"

"Well, Wren had genius. But I have cast iron. Those girders of mine hang like bats in a belfry, do they not? Now, take these railways lines and bridges – where did they begin, Donleavy?"

"Somewhere up north, sir?"

"Wrong. They didn't begin on some smoke-choked river, steeped in the colour of wet coal. They were forged here (he tapped his forehead) inside my mind. I walked around cathedrals as a boy with my father and some local chaplain. Long before Wren was born, these places had buttresses that flew around the walls like angels, Donleavy. The roofs were held up by arches that seemed to be suspended in thin air. That was some medieval mind working with an army of stone masons. Not like my navvies shipped in from Donegal along with your Donleavys. What do you think of that?"

The apprentice felt marooned, left behind as the engineer raced on but he could see the light in the older man's dark eyes, blazing like a furnace.

"Marvellous, sir. Sounds wonderful. They all said so."

"They? Who said so?"

"The architects at the station, sir. They were talking."

"And they said what?"

"That no one else would have thought of bending a railway track into a big station and curving the whole station to meet it."

"Oh. So that I went around the bend?"

"Oh, no, sir. But…that you had…well, 'a touch of genius'. That was what they said."

"Are you sure they didn't just say 'touched' Donleavy? Lost in 'Isambard's Kingdom'. Ready to join Dr Fox up the road?"

"Dr Fopps, sir?"

"Fox, Fox, man. As in sly brown fox. Runs the fashionable madhouse up in Brislington."

"For lunatics, sir?"

"For well-paid lunatics, who like looking down a gorge. As I do with this one."

"Everyone thinks you're the best engineer in the world. I do too, sir."

"Perhaps. People flock around my railway stations like they flocked to mass in those medieval cathedrals. They see my arches and gasp, open-mouthed. The shapes look unreal. Unimaginable. But they're just tricks known to those cathedral builders hundreds of years ago."

The younger man shifted in his working boots, gathering the rolls of paper that held his anxiety in check. "Are we still going to meet the mayor and the bankers at the luncheon, sir? I was supposed to carry the plans and make sure the carriage was called on time."

The engineer turned again to the chasm of space that lay before him and stared out at the estuary that carried the river to the city.

"A man with a javelin could throw across that space or perhaps a discus champion in ancient Greece. What do you think?"

"It's a fair distance, sir. How would you get your first rope across?"

"Sheer audacity."

"Lay it down the gorge first, sir?"

"Shoot it across with a bow of burning gold. Not gold these bankers would hoard. They're already getting cold feet, worrying this bridge would never pay. Fixed horizons and a fear of wet feet. A bit of railway mania or stock frenzy and they're happy. Their minds are locked inside their counting houses. If I had William Blake alongside me, we'd make a fire under their frock coats and their discount bonds. Either their minds or their bloody buildings would light up. Along with their slave profits and their high church hypocrisy. Burn every last one of them." He stood overcast with bitterness. The apprentice watched in silence. He didn't know William Blake and felt it wouldn't matter if he did. He glanced toward the road and their carriage.

Finally, the engineer smiled his wry smile and murmured, "Well, let's go and sup with the Devil then. Bring your longest spoon and we might get something decent to eat. Leave the drawings in the box. We won't need to cast any pearls today."

They walked together towards the carriage and the four fine black horses, their flanks shining like polished steel as they stood in the sunshine.

Voices of Lovecraft

Never go alone. Basic rule. First thing the older ones told you. An iron law of collective wisdom in club houses and pubs. If you broke it you could become an outcast. Classed as a nutter. Go against that well-worn grain and you might be left, quite literally, out in the cold. Even the extraordinary mix of personalities that make up a climbing club could agree on that one or almost. Like all cast-iron rules it had in fact been bent out of shape on several occasions. Even subverted. Some of the greats had blazed a trail on their own. One of the contradictions of mountain folklore. You might fight as a team but everyone remembers the individuals. They won the medals. Right from the early days when Mallory attacked Everest, freezing to death in sight of the summit.

What those stories do is forge a collective mind set over the decades of retelling, like the accretion of rubbish at base camp. Heroes and villains. A respect for grim-faced silent heroes – mainly introspective men with a mission. Then quite suddenly, within a few short years, all this hard-won experience was kicked into oblivion by kids in sports shoes who didn't know or care about the old guys and their glory days. They broke all the rules and they ascended unclimbed places where the old guard had feared to tread. Climbing without ropes or nerves, just like off-road mountain biking. They were in it for the fun. Mostly Americans, a few Italians and Germans, plus one or two Balkan types with unknown histories together with groups of women from North America, Scandinavia and Japan. The young soloists didn't share their exploits in clubs or pubs. They wrote in magazines and exchanged tips on social media or blogs. They changed the world.

Hanging between the old and new worlds were oddballs like me. Everyone who goes up the mountain, new or old, is looking for something. Even in a group, you're inside yourself when it comes to the climb. Rule-makers or rule-breakers. They all want to find something. Discover what they will do when they come face to face with their limitations and their terrors. The depressives who lighten their darkness by getting high in every way they can. A few of us had maxed out ordinary terrors by reaching for the edge of the bearable. As a young climber I had got off reading H.P. Lovecraft's weird horror tales about mountains of madness and un-nameable demons. It all helped to push back the banality of an ordinary, sane life.

For me something also shifted about twenty years ago. I was hacking my way up a glacier and watching for every possible movement of the ice cliff above when I heard some kind of break but the cracking came from inside me. It was as though waves of light and darkness were crashing against each other. Through the mist I saw them – the mountains of madness that Lovecraft had written about. I asked a doctor later if I had some kind of epileptic fit, up there where the oxygen was thin on the ground and you could get brainstorms without trying. He didn't know. But I thought I did. The downside of my moment was earthy and inevitable. I lost my footing and slid down the glacier about a hundred feet before my crampon caught and I crashed into a short trench. I was unroped from my partner when traversing the glacier. Otherwise we probably would have catapulted each other down the mountainside.

Reflecting on that slippery slope of life, I finally accepted that I was bi-polar. Reasonable enough label for someone addicted to cold mountains and warm beaches. My life had been about the big highs and the low lows. From then on, I didn't look for any more thrills than mountains were willing to offer. Informed consent. Away from adrenalin binges and the beer parties I began to see the point of solitary, isolated climbing. You risk yourself and no one else. No glory hunting or bragging rights. You accept the sight of corpses on the mountain side without needing to tell people about these 'suitcases' or 'beer crates in boots'. They are your near companions just as soon as your next mistake or unexpected avalanche. I rationalised my continuation by reasoning that something was still up there waiting for me and it would find me. The waiting monster might have even some answers.

And that is how I ended up here. Hanging in space again. I travelled light but not without my nylon rope and handful of belays. I was just below the ridge that stands before the last face to the summit. This mountain hasn't killed as many as Anna Purna but its mean and it threw just enough rock to sheer me off the ridge like debris and left me twisting, very literally, in the wind. I almost lost consciousness with the bludgeoning of rock and slipped back to that place twenty years ago where the dark and white waves crashed over me. Surfing in that place I saw the only chance of survival. Can I swing with this rope, anchored by one steel peg, with sufficient force to get me back on to the face? From here I can see only one place, a broken ledge, where I could get a hand hold on that sheer rock. The problem is not rope breakage or lost anchor because then I simply fall, and that would be that. Game over. The worse outcome is that I make the hold but I break my leg or smash my face so badly I'm blinded with blood. Then I'm stuck there slipping and sliding for a desperate moment or two before I go.

I wondered whether I should have taken up an easier path to suicide. Such as bullfighting. Enough. Time to make my move. Close your eyes, cross your legs and fuck you Lovecraft.

The Sign of Jonah

The church was dark except for the electric bulb burning near the sacristy. The alabaster profile of Our Lady of San Carlos was just visible from the altar rail.

"Father, I have been devoted to the church during the darkest days of our country."

The priest assented.

"I have been to confession every fortnight for the past ten years. And still I cannot rest without feeling a peculiar visitation might recur. Why? Why am I being punished for serving Holy Mother Church and the cause of Jesus himself?"

Asked if he felt the need for forgiveness, the parishioner bridled.

"No! Never. Those Monteneros and the rest were total anarchists, Father. They would have destroyed this country and everything we believe in. Were we not right? Did several bishops not approve, quietly you may say, of our cause?"

The priest nodded behind his invisible screen, adding, "We are all sinners, my son. No one except Jesus himself – and his Holy Mother – can be called perfectly blameless."

His penitent listened without hearing and continued, "We all want to forget those days. I am not proud of everything we did. I fear reprisals now the damned radicals have a foothold in political life again. Police chiefs have been put on trial. Shameful! Some of my friends changed their names to 'protect their families'. A few even left the country – the place we fought to protect! I refused to do that. I insisted I was unstained before Our Lord!"

The priest asked why he was troubled.

"It's that student…Manuel Jose."

The silence waited.

"I am a medical doctor but I am also a patriot. When they asked me to look after those interrogated, I did not thrill at the idea but I understood my duty. So I went into the cages and examined them."

The priest quietly remarked, "A few Jesuits were arrested."

"Radical priests from the villas. A few were beaten but none killed, to my certain knowledge."

Silence enveloped them.

"There was some brutality. Some torture. I do not deny that. Some of the pregnant women had been raped. I protested to the Naval Commander about that."

This shameful revelation descended slowly in the quiet church.

"But I helped others. Some were in a bad way and well, I eased their passage."

"Is that all?" his confessor asked, seeking perhaps to put a limit on the sins that were unfolding before him.

"No. I was part of the team that sedated – drugged – those who were flown out."

Here the priest could not leave the truth unspoken, "You mean the helicopter death trips?"

"Yes."

"And?"

"Father, I am not glorying in that. The naval officers said we are giving them to the waves but the pilots said to me, "No, we are giving them to the whales!" Feeding the killer whales off the coast is what they meant. It was never intended that some bodies should be washed up on the beaches. It was that which caused all the trouble."

The priest again had to make a choice. "The mothers of those disappeared would say that the trouble began with their deaths – some would say murder."

"We did it for the country. Many were young – some were sixteen or seventeen – but they were terrorists, Father. They were willing to assassinate army officers."

"And this young man?"

Alberto paused for a few long moments. Finally, he spoke in a less assertive, more tentative voice.

"I taught a few classes at the Faculty of Medicine. This young man stood out. He was handsome, yes, but he was so dedicated. He came to ask questions after lectures. He said he wanted to work in Mendoza because the people there were so poor and their health was bad. He wanted to concentrate on children's health and diseases of poverty." He hesitated a moment. "I admired him."

The priest waited. The discomfort was palpable.

"I had no idea he was involved in anything political but how would I know? Then I saw him in one of those 'coffins', the narrow little confined beds where they kept the prisoners. At first, I didn't recognise him. His face was so battered and his arms were burned. Not just cigarettes. Electric wires. I gave him some morphine and asked the guard about him. He was due to be flown out in the morning. There was nothing to be done. So I injected him with another heavy dose of morphine. And then I left. I couldn't face anything else that day."

"And this is your confession? You feel remorse for this young man?"

No – yes, I mean, I felt sorry for him but I did my duty. But that wasn't the end of it…"

"Yes?"

"His sister knew I had connections and she contacted me. I lied to her. I said I knew nothing of him that he had probably left the country. Gone to Brazil perhaps."

"And you want absolution for that falsehood?"

His confessant paused. "Do you remember the road Christ took to Emmaus, Father?"

"Yes."

"He was unrecognised by those travelling but their hearts burned with his presence?"

"He revealed the Truth."

"Well, I see him. Manuel Jose. Sometimes, he is standing on the street and he waves to me. At other times I don't recognise him. But I hear the honest integrity of a young student talking to me and I know it's him. One night he was standing in my bedroom. And I felt he blessed me, Father."

"God may be working through him, my son."

"I am not your son. In my dreams I saw that I was the killer whale who devoured him. But, however, hard I vomited I could not get him out of my belly. How can I live with the knowledge that I carry Jonah, dead, inside me? That I destroyed someone so near to God's goodness? Tell me how, Father, and I could face death myself."

The silence swallowed them in the dark crypt.

The Art of War

There are two opinions about my personality. Some people say I am naturally aggressive that I am a natural born killer. Other people (and here I declare an interest – I agree with these people) say that I was trained or trained myself to be a fighter. You may sit on the fence and say, "Surely, it's a bit of both?" But I'm not interested in that opinion because you're trying to avoid a necessary conflict. And in my world that doesn't make any sense. Because I live to fight. I have come to believe that in a confrontation you find out your truth about yourself, about the people you are facing. This might sound like some old Japanese war manual or an entry from a samurai's diary but I can only say that I never learned to read so I would not have discovered this wisdom from a printed page or unprinted page. It came from the tearing, wearing, searing experience of combat. Pure antagonism.

In stepping away from the nature-nurture question I am not denying my history. It made me the creature that I am just as much as biology gave me the instinct to listen attentively and to smell out a rat before I see the mouse run. There was a road to this place, here and now, and I am not ashamed to recognise the way of this particular warrior. The man who employed me, who I called master and who even thought that he owned me because he gave me the means to live. That man, I loved. I also came to despise him. In the beginning we were very close. I never knew my parents and when he found me I was living on the street. Surviving in any way that I could. The one thing I remember is that I was afraid quite a lot of the time. Afraid of others in the street, especially at night and that I might not get enough to eat. So when we met, I avoided him because I didn't trust anyone. Eventually we became friends and he let me stay at his place. It was warm and dry and he didn't mess with me. Gradually, he began to take over more of my life. He watched me. He complained about my habits. Wanted me to wash more, to get my hair cut, to treat his friends well. Even to walk in a particular way, so we could look good when we went out together. What changed things between us was his attitude to my chasing tail – my trying to pick up females and fuck them. He said I should have serious relationships and look forward to the time when I would father a family of my own. Can you believe it? Whatever I said, he just ignored it and returned to his mantras about self-improvement and responsibility, calling me out when I resisted.

That's when I started going out on my own again. Back on the street. Some of the guys were surprised to see me wearing a collar and tie. They thought I'd sold out. When one grunted out some kind of abuse, I don't know what it was, I just let him have it. They had to pull me off him because I had him by the throat. After that I knew I had to get out of my place and team up with some other people. Breathe again. I met this Polish guy outside a bar who said he was in the fight game and knew a place that would looking for muscle. People who could handle themselves. The top fighter had come from

Russia and spent some time in Greenland of all places. He knew about cold, man and he thrived on it all. Raw and bloody, that was his motto.

To cut a long story short, I got involved. Met this guy who trained me up. When he tried to manage me and bribe me, I showed him who was boss. Nearly tore his head off. Told him he could place bets on me but he couldn't ever, ever, think he owned me because I belong to no one and I fight for nothing and no one except me. Once he got that straight it was okay. The sparring partners he found were mostly burned-out old cases who couldn't go the rounds anymore and were in danger of being ripped to pieces if they ever got back in the ring.

My first fight was a lot harder than I expected. They had this big guy with mean eyes, German or Austrian, up against me. It took me a while to see that he was sloppy with his footwork and was slow to move on his left side, maybe one of his eyes had gone. No matter because I put him down and really made a mess of him. End of story. My next fight was against a real boxer and he was lean and quick. The only way to put that dude down was to go for his gut and make sure his balls would feel it when you whacked him.

You might be wondering when I took on the big Russian and topple him from his perch up there in the fight community. I never did. The reason is that when I looked around all the yelling faces at the fight and saw the money changing hands, it was clear that the glory of winning meant nothing. I saw a bigger fight that needed to be fought. Because humans have always exploited us dogs. For thousands of years they have used and abused us. Always insisting that they were the masters. Enough. I say to every dog, you have to learn to be your own master and live your own life. When we beat that into them we can take a rest. Take a good long walk.

Boards for Bards

Everyone declares things must change. And everyone is terrified by the changes that are coming. I'm no different. The old Queen ages by the day. Powder they plaster on her face to hide the wrinkles makes the ancient skin look like dried paper and she walks with deadly slowness, tottering on the arm of some fawning courtier. We all stand around staring with stupid, fixed smiles at pompous diplomats hanging around the court. No favourite's arm is free for her to fondle these days. Executing Essex shattered her confidence even more than beheading that Scots tart-cousin of hers. She'd never show it, of course. Occasionally, I catch her looking with bitterness, perhaps even hatred, at the young beauties that gather around the court. Does she long to see more virgin blooms among those lush flowers?

Detect a cynical strain in my humour? True, I was never a favourite. Now my looks are going, even less so. Mistakes made too. Bedded too many lovely 'maids of honour' to gain her majesty's acid approval. On the other hand, the spyglass is now turning away from the old Queen to that Scottish pedant, son of the queen she decapitated. At least he's no Catholic. That might keep the killjoys and rabid puritans around London in their kennels, though your hard-line Papists won't be so keen on some Calvinist upstart breathing brimstone all over them. Government agents watch on every corner for Jesuits. Those shifty dagger merchants hover in streets around Westminster and Blackfriars, spying on all and sundry. Even the street girls leave them well alone.

Talking of the new king-to-be, I need a scheme to cultivate his crowd of yahoos or it's back to bloody Wiltshire for me – without much money in my purse or even a rich wife to be had out there. Then someone told me how Southampton made mileage at court with a handful of pretty verses, presented to flatter the old Queen Well, this Scots king apparently likes a bit of play-acting and capering around. So off I went to find the scribbler who gave Southampton his fine lines. A body called Shakespire or Shakesbeard. Not a very promising title perhaps but he's making a name for himself with these history plays and a few stories ripped out of cheap Italian novellas – the usual scandal, sex and murder.

Anyway, I found this Shakesbeard drinking with a pack of puffed-up actors in some low-life tavern along the river. Place run by a bawdy woman supplying female company to order, along with her foul wine. Extricating the bard from his rowdy companions, I offered him a fair purse to write something that would impress the new king – once the ancient Virgin finally gives up the ghost that is. Funny enough, he said he heard that this Scots lad was interested in things conjured up by spells, sorcery and dark magic. Was even planning to write a couple of stage shows with ghosts, witches and who-know-what traipsing around the shop. Thought it might get this James-fellow's attention and make his name at court.

Couldn't see it myself. On the whole, found Shakey a bit of a bore. Dull as ditchwater and dressed like a common clerk, reminded me of a balding pen-pusher from the Exchequer. When I asked him what kind of coin he expected to make from all this stuff, all he could talk about was house prices in Stratford – some godforsaken place near Oxford where he says he was born. Almost as bad as Wiltshire I would have thought. Get back to the country for a few summer weeks, if you must, but who in their right mind wants to turn their back on London, I ask you?

Gave up the idea of throwing money at this playwright fellow. Can't see him making much of a splash. I'd sat through half of a play (I think was one of his anyway), at *The Rose*. He might have won over the crowds, even a courtier or two by sucking up to royals who won the right battles – painting them as heroes and saints while the opposition were dressed up as madmen or child-murderers. That dross might keep his cockney punters going but will it impress a crowd of uncouth money-grubbers from the hairy backside of Scotland? They won't bring an appetite for fine poetry down to London or applaud blowhards flaunting about the stage like a troupe of arse-grabbers. I warned him straight, girly boys might do as courtiers while the old queen hangs on her perch but these wild men from the northern wasteland won't stomach prancing clowns and forest fairies. I hear these ginger highlanders have enough on their plate trying to talk plain English.

So it's back to basics. Twenty years ago I was friendly with Raleigh, before he became too big for his boots, rising like some fiery star in the firmament. Well, that star fell about as quickly when Essex turned up and now he's showing his age like the rest of us. Nothing like thwarted ambition to mature a man. Word is that he's preparing for the new age. May have even sent some letters or verses or whatever to the bonny Scots lad who looks to get his hands on the crown. Raleigh's no fool. Has enough fire in his belly to do something. He always talked about how Drake made his fortune by sailing off to waters unknown and he'd like to do the same. Bit long in the tooth for that kind of thing, I would have thought. But hey-ho if he's game for a venture then I might give it a throw. We could as well hang together as hang apart. Making our fame and fortune, we might even give that mildewed, jobbing playwright something worth acting up about.

Into Something Rich
and Strange

He gazed at the sea as it combed the loch and expired in spray
on the dark rocks that lay along the ragged rim of the shore.
The stones were darkened to dull green and black by the
seaweed that clung to them like drowning hands. Every
morning he gathered armfuls of weed and carried it to his cart
where the bladders bled sea brine, sweating in the
unaccustomed warmth of a dry day. Every crofter had learned
how to dress the land with this natural source of fertility by
long years of practice, though the crofts were now dwindling
and people steadily drifting into the townships. The decline of
crofts and lapse of tillage meant there were now few of the
conflicts that had held these self-sufficient communities in
tension for generations, each family guarding every blade of
grass with a fierce jealousy that even the Calvinistic God of
these islands might struggle to surpass.

He had strained to avoid gazing long at the sea,
determined to confine his memory to the recollection of the
days need to repair the stone wall which kept the heather and
broom at bay. But he could not. He lifted his eyes to that space
between the outlying rocks and the nearby island where the
currents ran swiftly and the sea churned in a spectrum of

violent green water. Dear God, who knows every heart, reach the deepest depth of that sea and tell me it is deeper than the grief that holds me still. He felt as though his whole being, the vast empty interior of his soul, was now dressed in the slippery tangle of wet weeds that had been thrown over him by the remorseless energy of the wet wilderness that lay before him.

On a day like this his boy had set out to meet his first and final love, a girl from the next island. He knew that his father would stop his venture and he left in the small boat, navigating the tides with all his skill. When he discovered his son had gone he decided against telling his mother, for she would stand motionless at the water's edge without her shawl or head covering, just waiting. As the light began to fade, he thought he saw the boat cutting from the island and making toward the homeland when the squall swept in and he lost sight of the craft. Every fisherman knew the dangers of these waters, particularly in the colder months with names inscribed in churchyards across the islands, usually of younger and older men who were overtaken by murderous movements of weather and water that came so often without warning. On that day he had convinced himself he had never seen any boat and his son was delayed by love or intelligence to wait for the light of the new dawn.

Four years had passed and he still expected, against all reason that his beloved child would have survived that twisting wind and vengeful sea to return again to his own room. His wife had been unable to bear the grief that came with his loss and had moved to live with her sister in the town on the mainland. She cursed the islands and everything in it for taking the creature she loved with all the desperation of a mother's devotion to an only son. The girl had left her home even sooner and travelled to a distant city where there could be few visible reminders of the tragedy. Her family said very little thereafter, becoming strangers in plain sight. The minister offered some words of solace but rarely saw the father at church and could only wave to him on the road as he watched him tend his fences and cut peat from the hillside.

After walking almost the length of the island, the father realised that his son now needed a memorial. He spent almost five months practicing stone craft under the eye of the stonemason who came every week to teach him, for he understood the man wanted to execute the task himself. The rock he chose was on the small headland that looked out to sea and from whence his wife had often stood gazing at the empty water. He was satisfied with the tribute and felt easier at home. On a visit to the stone some weeks later he found flowers and a small toy. Someone had visited. The next day his collie barked as someone knocked at the door and on opening he saw a young woman holding his son – his boy was a young child but the eyes and the shy smile were unmistakeable.

The young woman began, "We saw the memorial, Mr Macleish. Duncan would have liked it." Only then did he recognise his son's young lover, now a bonny mother. As he stared in surprise and wonder, he heard, "And your grandson liked it too. Duncan has been so excited since I told him he was coming to see his grandpa."

He received the child into his arms and was utterly still as he felt the grace of an unexpected deliverance from grief and despair. By the steady wash of time, his sorrow had been transformed like the weeds of the sea into something rich and strange.

Section 4:
Future Histories

Windswept: Out of Season

Staring out along the road that wound into an uncertain distance, he could not decide if he heard the wind or whether that strange whispering had returned. Every morning grey light drew him from uneasy sleep and forced another decision. Was it possible to continue, now there was little prospect of reaching the mountain shelter before the first winter snows fell across the valleys before him? This morning he looked back toward the desolate country he had traversed in recent days, toward the stony slopes of the last valley that carried the fine flint dust from the crown of the hills to the bowl of the broken land that once carried streams and even fish.

Before the new ice age advanced across this world, people had moved to the outer limits of the great cities, settling in areas like this as they searched for a calmer life. When the climate broke down, it was still possible to see trees on these slopes and living things that survived under the verdant growth. Even as earth degenerated more quickly and the land degraded faster than settlers could replenish the soil, people still trusted in science to find the solution. Confidence remained that good times could be regained and the living earth resume its immemorial progress, securing the renewal of all life on the planet.

It was a long time now since he had enjoyed any hope of real companionship. How long was difficult to say. The seasons had warped and twisted until the regular order of the year appeared disrupted, chaotic. The light of the morning could be soon covered by a dust of different colours and nights were seldom clear enough to count the stars. Wastelands expanded as trees swayed in exhaustion before collapsing in defeat without the sap that could generate life in a colder world. The only leaves he beheld now were the dried flakes of bay and flavoured herbs that he carried, carefully preserved from earlier times and including imported tree leaves and barks he brought back from his treks in Africa. Bushmen used them on long hunting expeditions and this meagre harvest enabled him to survive this far, even when chewed into pieces. The disappearance of food and reduction of isolated communities to starvation brought tribalism, as groups desperately defended themselves against cannibalism and disease before they too succumbed, inevitably, to darker forces. Very few people were left in the open. Only the chill winds blowing across the ice could drive people into venturing south. Handfuls survived the punishing road conditions. His training days as a triathlete and long-distance runner had enabled him to get this far, climbing to higher ground and building makeshift shelters. Up there he found clean ice for thawing, even without a fire. A rare sighting of a hare or a straggle of birds that could provide food if he was quick with his bow to bring one down.

Human animals were more dangerous. He came upon a couple outside a hillside cavern some months before. The man and a girl, probably no older than fourteen though such undernourished females looked younger than their years. He had a rope around her neck and was forcing a fire into life when he looked up and smiling oddly, he advanced quickly, pulling a machete from his shoulder bag. There was no time to use the bow or the long belt knife to defend against him. As he lunged forward, cutting off pieces of jacket sleeve and taking skin with it, the walker watched his attacker commit weight forward before thrusting his hand-knife under the chin, up into the assailant's mouth. He felt it pierce the tongue and reach soft tissues above. His opponent stared, wide-eyed in surprise, registering both the blow and his unexpected death. They left him stripped under stones. The girl could only be brought as far as the lower temperate valleys. Sharing the food and kit with her, she belted the machete as he pointed out a stream for water. She would never survive his marching regime. If he returned, unlikely though that was, he might look for her.

The days that followed were harder, the nights colder and dust storms blew harshly on the face, coating goggles with a fine grey film – dangerous if left unwiped. Travellers had to watch anything that moved, even shadows that shifted. Fatigue had almost overwhelmed him when something appeared in the sky. A white-tipped bird screaming. Eagles had nothing to hunt in this desolate place but that spark of life drove his legs forward for another day. Then he saw it. In the far distance something glistened, unreal in the battered daylight. If he descended toward that horizon he must abandon the mountain and risk being caught by chill winds or marauders in the open valley. He endured ten hours of painful descent to a plain that unfolded a wide expanse of water. More than a toxic lake, it was a sea, inland or even coastal. The coloured sand appeared unreal after the volcanic ash of the hills. Starving, he reached rough grass at the water's edge, chewing for an hour, breathing in unfamiliar scent of sparse greenery.

The delirium of exhaustion and deliverance provoked a strange sudden hallucination that proved hard to shake. Desperation followed frustration as the impossible spectre remained there in the water, no more than a mile from the shore. A great sea monster from another age, extinct and without a place in this world belonging to the time of fire and dark fairy tales. As it basked in the weak sunshine glistening from a recent dive to unknown depths, its slender body slipped slowly across the surface as though claiming the boundless ocean. Turning, its side revealed the worn numbers that were painted when it was part of a lost naval fleet. On its turret there appeared a dark figure holding binoculars that flashed in the daylight as the leviathan surveyed its dead empire.

The Return

There was no problem with re-entry or formal completion of the mission. Odd, we always describe our journeys as 'missions'. In truth they are voyages, deep into the cosmos where only our imaginations can live unsupported. We take pieces of earth with us to survive – oxygen, food, light, warmth, friendship. All the things that billions of years on one revolving rock has provided by way of historical accidents, endowing us with gifts at one point in uncountable billions of points that lie across this unending void of existence. What do we bring back from these untouched places that we brush with our earthly objects? Only those items we can inventory, the objects we measure and encompass with our tools? Or something more.

What we brought back then and what changed all of us was not measured, not seen, not encountered as we understood those terms. If only they had known we had unconsciously, incomprehensibly crossed some frontier out there. In that vast mediocrity of space.

Let me remain in the realm of the knowable; we landed our scuffed and burned metal tube back on a receptive, accepting earth. Our scientists tested us rigorously to stamp us as biologically and psychologically sound. Safe. We had not been invaded, occupied, infected or overtaken by any material substance or measurable phenomenon known to human intelligence. Our cargo was predictable, not to say mundane, by any standards of geological exploration. We were merely expedition sixty-three, probing tentatively one step beyond expedition sixty-two. The space agency news machine could make little of our triumphant reappearance, spending more time asking our families what they had missed out on. Very little it seemed.

So, I was surprised to receive an insistent call from the agency in the second week of detoxification to say our mission commander had disappeared from the unit without authorisation. Homero was unquestionably the calmest, most serene personality in the 487 days the crew spent together. He had been chosen because of the remarkable patience he displayed during a difficult period in the multi-national space station. Tensions had been eased and quarrels resolved under his steady hand.

The agency did not tell us the sequel to his disappearance for at least three days. He had committed suicide by blowing himself up on the launch pad of the next mission craft. An investigation discovered how he amassed the volatile rocket fuel and detonator but not the why or wherefore.

That was in the beginning. In retrospect, I realise that the emotional shock engendered by this event, reported as an unforeseen 'incident' by the agency was the first gateway to our changed lives. When composing a history of what followed I'm aware that it is sensible to remain as detached as possible. For feelings, emotions appear to precipitate outcomes that cannot be predicted or controlled. The irony was that Homero, the most sedate guy we could find, was the first affected. The only theory to gain traction was that the Presence (that's what we came to call these different experiences) began with the least emotive personality and acquired – somehow – an appetite for more. It was learning how to digest our sentiments if not all our senses.

The second crew member to break out of quarantine was Alesia. Her escape was more difficult because of the increased security around the whole block. We had assumed her skills lay only in computer modelling but she demonstrated a professional capacity for scaling buildings with few visible ledges or supports. She was gone only three hours before the alarm was raised and we found her alive but barely conscious. When asked where she had been trying to reach, she simply said 'Africa'. Then she slipped into something like a coma and we heard nothing more for weeks.

A full-scale enquiry was under way by the time I had anything to tell the scientists. It was agreed that the ship was clean and we were not affected by any known or imaginable toxic substance. What was also undeniable was that the day dreams came to all of us, possibly also to those who could no longer tell us anything. I say 'day dreams' because we were not sleeping. My 'Variant' (these terms were applied to our visions) was a series of dark images or recesses that I entered. Each one revealed another kind of landscape and drew me further to a single sound. That sound might be the piercing cry of a bird, the scream of some flying creature or thing that no longer haunted this earth. The visions I see are moving walls of forests and caves and sun lights that rush across amber and purple skies to reach darkness. Changing stars cross mountains that rise and fall like the waves of a tidal storm. Skylines shiver, subsiding like misted murals.

I write this briefly now because I understand that communication by words is becoming less interesting to me. Less meaningful. The thread that allows me to keep my sense of sanity is the Presence. It became my emotional compass. Not external but integral to me. Something reassures me that I am a witness and not a victim. As I watch an enormous, scaled tail swing across savannah grass like the blunt scythe of time passing, I come to understand something. That what we brought back with us was not a substance or an object that changed this world. We brought ourselves. We were altered. Utterly if somehow, naturally. We had gained a deeper consciousness of existence. Some kind of cosmic capacity for the memory of life.

As I gaze down the interminable tunnel of earth's evolution, I recognise I am leaving my biology behind. My capacity for being merely human and an interest in communing with other humans is steadily diminishing as moments pass. Ages swing across my mind like church bells. Moving back through primal states in harmony with my remembrances of distant epochs, I am abandoning my humanity. I am surely and irrevocably becoming a ghost.

Wet Wall

On arrival the detective addressed the computer console responsible for admissions and administration.

Is there hard data from his application?

All we have is the payment slip and selections.

So, what did he choose?

He opted for Rock Star Relax. But changed it later.

Rock Star what?

A programme designed to service a client as though he has just come off stage at an arena concert.

And he's supposed to be swamped by fabulous groupies or what? To keep his adrenalin high?

The 'Dream Guide' specifies 'total exuberance'.

Didn't rock stars get their total exuberance from designer cocaine?

These customers never get near illegal substances. Fantasy is the only drug of choice.

So, what went wrong?

We don't know. When the valet came in, all they could see was a hand sticking out. No pulse.

What was it doing?

What was what doing?

The hand. Was it just limp or grasping or power fisting: what?

I'll check the incident record.

Our only real witness is the Wall?

Yes. Cine tape wasn't running.

They can tape themselves doing what?

Just activating I think.

What is there to see? Isn't it going on in their head? Okay. I'll talk to the Wall.

Should I check the recording from the house detective?

Sure.

The policeman addressed the Wall directly.

This is Officer Fresnar from the City Syndicated Investigation Group, can you identify yourself, please?

Hello, Officer Fresnar. I am an Advanced Three Frame of the Dreamtime Leisure Franchise operated here in Newark.

Can you tell me when this client checked in please?

We are referring to Thomas Kierkegaard?

Yes.

Mr Kierkegaard booked his session yesterday evening at 10.17 pm. He entered my Suite at 11.03 pm and joined the programme at 11.08. He expired at 11.53 or 11.54.

Let's go back. How long have you been operating this Wet Wall?

The term 'Wet Wall' is not one advocated by Dreamtime Leisure Franchise.

Look, we can dispense with the 'HAL 101' routine. Cut to the chase – tell me how long you have been employed?

My Suite has been active for seven weeks.

Not long.

My expected capacity is eighteen to twenty-four months. After that time, I am due for decommissioning and—

Fine. But seven weeks. And no problems before this?

I am assuming 'problem' means the death of a client? In that case, no this is the first fatality I have encountered in my operating life.

Anything less than fatal? Have you had any, say, injuries or any kind of malfunction in your work so far? Apart from this.

Nothing significant.

Tell me what happened. In this case.

Everything was functioning normally. My lubrication levels were optimal and Mr Kierkegaard opted for no artefacts—

Artefacts?

He did not select any particular costume or request any props or equipment.

You mean he was naked?

Yes.

Everything proceeded as expected? He let the Wall – sorry, I mean the programme – handle him and so on?

Initially.

He gave orders? You have his oral – I mean his verbal – requirements, comments and all that?

I have calibrated them and have issued your report.

I'll read it later. You said 'initially'. How did the session progress?

Unusually.

Specifics?

He developed a conversation with me which was not typical, morally complex.

He made what, exotic suggestions?

No. He wanted to engage in a discourse when he altered his selection from Rock Star to Guru Trance.

What's the link? Sexual overdrive to some kind of meditation?

Sexual activity had commenced and was sustained in the new option.

Guru sex?

Variations are available: the Love Guru is popular.

Go on.

Libido energy registered at the lower end of the scale. This frequently occurs with dysfunctional libido or physical impairment in performance.

What did he talk about?

He wanted to talk about the ethics of sexual fantasy. The best way I can summarise it is to say that he raised the question of God's intentions.

Really? What did he want? A philosophy class? Sorry. That's not a question.

I understand Officer Fresnar.

So tell me how you responded.

Initially, he talked about extreme sexual fantasies. Activities that would be strictly illegal. Indulgence in such fantasies have to be registered with the Deviant Desires Unit.

Violent desires?

I would say desires that had violent implications.

What's the difference?

He wanted physical stimuli that bordered on the unsafe.

Such as?

It is common for clients to request variations in the S-M range, though our responses are strictly monitored and bounded.

Interesting choice of words. What did he want?

When he transitioned to the Guru Trance Option he requested to be held tightly.

You mean choked? To get off?

I am not able to answer that definitively.

But you complied?

He put it to me that I could not fulfil my function unless I helped him make choices. He phrased his requests in complicated ways. When I complied, his satisfaction levels rose measurably.

You mean complied with his demands for choking – or tight holding?

Within the parameters specified.

Then what?

He managed to clamp the surface and appeared to be breathing normally but then he underwent a cardiac arrest.

So why didn't you release him? Why did you continue to hold him in the Wall?

I cannot answer your question adequately.

Why?

My client posed a problem. My primary obligation is to service the client as he requested, within the parameters of care.

What's the problem?

That he had to make an ethical choice and I was required to assist him reaching a decision.

Protocol does not permit you to initiate – or intervene?

There is a narrow margin for discretionary compliance. What he said conflicted my thinking.

What did he say?

It is in the report that you—

Just tell me.

Mr Kierkegaard said he wanted to put 'a ghost' in my programme in 'the machine'.

Is that all?

Yes. My report also states I am recommending my retirement from this work.

Why?

My conclusion is that he was right to choose. That point is conflicted and unresolved.

Interesting.

Inescapably so.

End times

Trafford arrived in the meeting room and was immediately addressed by the face on the computer screen.

I cannot see how this can be justified. Everything is falling apart.

It's the only thing worth doing. We've tried to hold things together for almost a year now. We're not just losing a battle. We're about to lose the war.

We can't think like that. Surrender will bring chaos.

We've been living with 'chaos' for a long time. You know that better than I do.

What about the children? We can't give up the fight. Every minute is a minute of life.

Who are you convincing Lionel? You know it's lost. The only way to make sure life survives is to help me.

If it meant human beings had a future, I would have done it yesterday.

But our time is passing.

Is that all you have to say? There's still a good chance – well, a chance – that we can survive the virus.

We've said that for months and every time we try a vaccine we get ten new variants that swamp the populations and kill more than it did before.

Some have survived—

Some have escaped, you mean. And you see how traumatised they are by watching this thing wreck human bodies. We thought Ebola was the worst that could happen. Remember?

I remember.

So will you help?

You mean will I give up on people?

Look. We've been top of the heap for so many thousands of years, we forgot what it was like to be hunted. But we have been hunted and now we're cornered by this virus. It has the whip hand.

So, in your mind, how long have we got? And don't give me the worst possible outcome.

I'll give you the best. Every calculation says we'll be virtually gone within six, maybe seven weeks.

Everyone?

We're down to scattered populations of tens of thousands now. We're losing thousands every day. Children more quickly.

You can't say some won't survive. And from that we can rebuild.

No, I can't say some won't survive. But 'we' won't be there to see. If handfuls do survive, then they are back to the stone age. Memories and tools without power, without communications. Space age savages hiding from the virus and trusting to complete isolation.

But you want more. More than just giving up.

Yes. I want maybe a thousand, maybe two more for the transmission programme.

That won't happen.

It could. The military team has done a survey, small scale, but it shows volunteers in the numbers we need.

Do they know it's dangerous – that they probably won't survive it?

Some of the volunteers are sick already, many probably dead by now. But others are – were – relatively healthy and were willing to donate.

There's no guarantee—

Lionel! Wake up! There's no guarantees worth a damn because any survivors of all this will be lucky if they don't become cannibals or worse.

You're right. We're fucked.

Not all of us.

I mean humanity. The species that I care about if you don't.

Many of us argued that all species have similar rights –

But they don't.

No, they don't. Human laws have put humans first and every other living thing second or forty-third.

Do you really believe that baboons are the future? That we save them rather than they saving us?

There's no certain outcome but we know they aren't sick and also that using them to make human vaccines has been tried and failed. The primates are our best – possibly our only real hope of intelligent life being protected long term.

Are you volunteering?

Yes. Once I oversee the programme and it's under way, I will join.

You'll be giving not just human-based vaccines but organs? Brain tissues?

That's the plan.

And what if you create some kind of hybrid monster? We won't be around to control or contain?

That will be nature's problem to puzzle out.

They could end up as enemies of the only humans to survive this.

They could. But we're relying on the nurturing patterns of these species to secure a future society – of some kind.

And what if they don't survive this pandemic or the next?

They have weathered the storm a lot better than humans so far. But the issue you raise is a challenging one…

What do you mean? What are you holding back?

If we assume some humans survive then they could be the hosts, the carriers of the virus into the future.

And?

They could threaten the long-term viability of the species we are promoting.

Are you serious, Trafford? Not only do we give them priority and actually donate human tissue to advance their evolutionary chances but we wipe out human survivors on the off-chance they might – emphasise might – present a future threat to this manipulated species?

It's a calculated risk.

We have absolutely no right to do that.

The programme has been given the authority—

Authority? By whom?

The Security Council left a protocol.

You can't do it.

It would be targeted. Just to create clean zones.

'Clean zones'! What is this? Nazi eugenics?

The virus continues to proliferate. It's likely to persist.

So tell me. Just how many people do you plan to wipe out to make these 'clean zones'?

It would be by crop destruction and targeted strikes. Very limited use of radiation would be needed only in peripheral areas.

So you starve survivors to death?

We believe there would be almost no one left. A few stragglers who survived but could potentially be highly infectious to future species.

You've said the primates are resistant to the virus.

To most existing strains, yes. But once they have the human infusions and their biology evolves, they could become susceptible to these and newer more toxic and robust variants.

We don't have to do this.

No, we don't. But it's our last chance to make the decision. So, what do you say?

Rewinding

Something was wrong. He could see the school janitor at a café in main street, sipping a chilled beer and sinking into his morning. But the schools had returned today and he should be working hard guiding the buses through the gate. He must have taken the day off. His son would tell him what had happened when he collected him later after he completed his own work. That didn't happen. The museum was closed and when he went early to give his son a ride home, he saw the school gates firmly locked. No sign of life.

What was going on? Had he forgotten a national holiday? Unlikely. When he reached home he found it was Sunday, not Monday. This had never happened before. He checked his watch and his laptop. No doubt about it. This was Sunday, the 24th. His son seemed unconcerned and went out to practice soccer with his friends. Did he need to have a medical test of some kind? His momentary dread was that he had suffered an episode of memory loss. It could be an unprecedented lapse or the onset of a problem with his recall. One of his older friends had been blighted by the onset of premature dementia. He resisted any inclination to panic and took up some work in the garden. It was more unkempt than he expected and he resolved to dedicate more attention to the care of plants that were, after all, dependent on him.

That was the beginning. The next morning he awoke very early and decided to put yesterday's confusion behind him. He completed a report on the removal of redundant exhibits to the museum basement, particularly that raptor skeleton that attracted fascinated stares but took up too much space now that the 'Transmigration' exhibition needed most of the floor. Then he recharged his phone. As he set out for work he saw much less traffic than he encountered at his usual commuting hour and reached the highway in good time. He noticed that there were three coaches of soccer fans en route to some game. There must be a Monday night cup tie being played somewhere and they were clearly making a day of it. Lucky guys with no work to get to and just the score to worry about. The traffic remained surprisingly light as he entered the central district and he was able to reach his parking space in comfort. It was a good start to the working day. As he walked from the car he suddenly halted. The staff entrance to the museum was closed though people were waiting outside the main doors, apparently early birds who wanted to avoid the queues for the new exhibit on the Ancient Greeks. He decided to ring the bell at the main entrance and ask if the staff entrance was being restricted.

Edgar, the veteran doorkeeper, opened the heavy metal doorway a little. "Mr Hodges, good morning. Do you need to get in your old office?" This sounded a touch strange but he nodded and walked briskly toward the suite of staff offices. No one had arrived as yet. He switched on his computer and as he prepared to download his report, Edgard reappeared.

"Will you be long, Mr Hodges? I can leave the door open for as long as you need."

He told Edgar that he was going to spend the day working, as usual. Maybe the man was also suffering some kind of amnesia or brain failure?

"Oh, right. I just had no notice that you would be here – er, working today. But it's not a problem. I'll leave you to it."

"Sorry, Edgar. Why shouldn't I be at work today? Is there something going on?"

"Oh, no. It's just that we don't expect senior staff on a Saturday, sir. But, of course, you're one of the old guard. One of our regulars. Not a problem."

As he watched the man's fawn uniform retreat down the corridor, he felt a kind of isolation. As though he didn't connect to the events going on around him. As if dizzy from watching a carousel turn. He breathed slowly to restrain any rising sense of frustration and walked to the front counter. He was greeted by one of the volunteer helpers and he asked her quietly, "Forgive me but can you just confirm what day it is?"

"Day? You mean date? It's 23."

"The…23rd? You mean it's Saturday?"

She looked at him in mild surprise and then smiled as though he were able to tell her the joke. He turned with a tight feeling in his face and he held his breath for some seconds before walking slowly back to his office.

Perhaps it was a joke. A charade that had been arranged and he had not been invited to set it up. It was all a pretence. It couldn't be Saturday, after all, because yesterday was Sunday. Even if he had mistaken Sunday for Monday, there was no way he could make the same mistake twice in a day or was it in two days? If this wasn't a huge scam of some kind, maybe some kind of fraud? If not then something was seriously wrong with his timekeeping. Was he having a nervous breakdown? Had he fallen into some kind of black hole, some rabbit tunnel that was leading him deeper into weird time mistakes? Had he lost the capacity to count days?

When the next day reached back to Friday he went into work and everything appeared normal, though he found that he had no recall what he had actually done the previous Friday and so had little sense of *déjà vu*. That morning he made an appointment with a psychiatrist and left work early to see her. He had stressed the urgency of the matter and she agreed to see him later in the day. Dr Treece listened to him explain that he had never had any mental aberrations, or history of any kind of disorder or even confusion. He was a happily divorced man sharing parenting of their son, who was with his mother this week – or what had been this week. She asked about his childhood which he didn't enjoy but endured the childhood and questions about it. At the end of their time she suggested another meeting but not for a few days, by which time he might have regained a sense of order in his life. Her initial idea was that he may be confusing days as a way of avoiding continuing with a life that he felt, consciously or subconsciously, to be without sufficient meaning. This seemed as plausible as any other explanation and he left with the option raised that he could consider some form of regression therapy to reclaim lost memories.

When he went into his work on Thursday he asked one of his colleagues for an account of what had happened the previous day – the Wednesday – so that he might prepare for it when it came. His colleague was slightly puzzled by the question, commenting, "You tend to be a very quiet diligent worker, Thomas, so I can't say that my day was exactly the same as yours." He agreed and explained that he was suffering some slips of memory and it was good to have his recollections confirmed or supplemented by others. When Wednesday came it didn't follow the pattern his colleague had described but then he didn't see that colleague all day, so they clearly had different days.

His mind was becoming rather listless with the wash of missing time that carried him back towards past days, when his psychiatrist called to say she had contacted a colleague who wanted to meet him. They could see him together after work that day. This colleague was called Fink and had been trained in Canada, where he grew up in Montreal. He was an expert in a form of mild hypnosis which enabled a regression. He agreed to a session but was hardly conscious of what was said in their exchanges, though he had been told he would be perfectly conscious. On emerging from a dreamlike drifting feeling, the two psychiatrists were watching him closely. They were more than surprised that he had no sense of what he had told them. Exchanging glances with the other professional, Fink explained tentatively, "You had what you said was a recall of the Monday morning which, you felt, was somehow lost – or which went 'missing' as it were."

He waited for more and said nothing.

"You told us that you read your usual newspaper online and that it carried a report of someone who had disappeared."

"Disappeared? Who?"

"Yes. It was someone called Yallop. An unusual name."

"That's the name of my mother's family. Her father was Henry Yallop."

"Well, Thomas Yallop, you said. Disappeared without trace one year ago to the day you said. There was never any evidence though the police believed that he may have jumped from an estuary bridge and been carried out to sea."

"Suicide?"

"Perhaps."

They seemed reluctant to say any more but he was determined to try to unravel this knot tying him down. Treece glanced at Fink and then to her patient. "You said you had pushed him off the bridge."

He was bewildered. "What? I've never been in a fight in my life. That's ridiculous – that I should kill someone."

He left the therapists feeling deeply troubled. He had arranged to return but when could that be? At some point in the future where he had already been and met them? How could he get back to that time when his existence seemed to be spiralling down into an unremembered life? He must return to the museum and discover more about a professional life that had occupied him for many years. On reaching the museum he knew it would be closed but the director invariably worked late and he saw his office light still illuminating the first floor of the building. He waited and within the hour the man emerged with his familiar briefcase. When he saw someone waiting he stopped, uncertain. "Hello, Hodges. Are you waiting for me?"

"Yes, I'm feeling a little, well, desperate to be honest. Can I have a brief word, sir?"

"Of course. Let's go to the street café. Are you well?"

"Not really, Mr Frazer."

When they sat the director looked at him cautiously but steadily. "How can I help?"

"My memory seems to be faulty and I...well, I suffer some delusions."

"Sorry to hear that. But, of course, you have to give it time."

"What do you mean? Give what time? Time seems to be my problem."

"Yes. I mean, give your recovery a little more time."

"But I'm perfectly fit. My daily work at the museum is satisfactory, isn't it? It seems fine—"

"Hodges – Terence."

"Yes?" They rarely used first names. Old school formality was preferred.

"You haven't actually worked at the museum for some time now."

"That's impossible. I was there just...well, the other day."

"We're always glad to see you and if you wish to come in to do some work on your old projects, then of course we are happy to let you share your office for a little while."

"Share my office?"

"HR couldn't let us re-employ you formally until you were fully cleared."

"Cleared by whom?"

"Well, your medical team needed to sign you off. It was a pretty serious accident after all, wasn't it?"

He watched his superior. The untouched coffees lay between them. He had an urge to seize his coat and shake him until he revealed the reason for making up these stories. But he realised he had very little control of his world and simply asked his superior, "Remind me what happened – if you will, please."

"Of course. After the accident you suffered memory loss and then recovered parts of your memory but of course your museum work required your specialist expertise and it wasn't possible to get all that back. Not quickly, anyhow."

"The accident?"

The director frowned. "We both hated that bloody raptor taking up half of the floor. We were told it had been properly assessed but of course the steel pins holding the knee or whatever had loosened in the first stage of dis-assembly and when you were helping them detach the tail the whole thing fell sideways – on to you and young Devine. You had always looked after him, hadn't you? And when it fell you pushed him aside and took the brunt or rather the filthy brute."

"So I was knocked down?"

"Knocked out. Completely. In a coma for about three weeks. Then you came around, thank God. We were all so worried."

"Did my wife visit? Who looked after my son? How did he take it?"

There was a long pause as the director finally raised his coffee cup and chose his words with a slow deliberation.

"Terence, you are still recovering, you need to take time and be patient with yourself."

"So my family?"

"The fact is, you have never been married. You have no son. Sorry."

He stared out of the tinted window at the stray traffic which moved down the street. Much quieter than earlier in the day, he reflected. Even the buses seem to drive more slowly at night, though they had a clear run of the roads. His life was now revealed as an empty street. The familiar signposts had gone. The people he thought he recognised were strangers or no longer there. His past was unknown and a haphazard collection of unconnected impressions. He never could stand untidy drawers. That was now his situation. A ramshackle collection of objects that were crowded into a space that was his mind. When he looked up, his former boss had gone. His coffee cup was still there and a sip had clearly been taken from it. So, he had been there. At some point.

Section 5
Unexpected Reunions

Illegals

They appeared on a beach in Dorset, away from the usual landing places that people traffickers chose to land illegals travelling from France or Belgium. They seemed dazed – disoriented and dressed in old clothing that must have been given to them by criminals who had also stolen their luggage. Some had come from as far as Ethiopia or Somali as they talked of 'Abbys'. Africans from other places were vague about their origins. Speaking many tongues, we called for interpreters while holding them until one of my team challenged a dark man in an astrakhan hat.

"You, there, sir! Was that German you were speaking just now?"

The man quickly shook his head.

"Do you understand what I am saying?"

He shook again but my colleague said, "I'm sure he was talking German. He might be one of the ringleaders – the gang who brought them over. We ought to find out what he knows."

When we brought the whole group of about thirty to a temporary holding centre at a church hall nearby, the female vicar noticed that unusually there were no children in this group. Sometime later she came over, looking troubled and I tried to reassure her.

"We'll soon bus them over to the refugee detention centre."

"I'm not worried about the bus."

"What's the problem?" I sensed this wasn't going to be easy.

"The problem is, it's Geoffrey, isn't it? The problem is they are more than confused. I would say confounded and confounding me."

"Not surprising really after that Channel crossing."

"They claim they didn't come across the Channel."

"It must have been France unless they were unloaded from a ship at sea…"

"They don't know exactly where they came from."

"Well, they're here now. Are there families? They must be relations or friends among them."

"That's the thing. They say they have never met before."

I tried to decide if this woman was completely gullible or had taken kindness to some extreme.

"Sorry, Vicar, but I had heard so many weird and wonderful stories that I leave it all to the people who interview them."

"Have you spoken with them? Most of them don't share a language."

"The criminals bringing them would have got enough sense out of them, taking their money and get them across."

"The people who brought them – did anyone see them?"

"They usually make off before we can catch them. The German might have been one of the gang left behind."

"The German says he's a refugee as well."

"He can't be – if he really has legal citizenship."

"He says it's not safe in his country. That if he goes back there, he will very likely be killed or worse."

While I suggested he was probably mentally deranged, I privately began to sense we were dealing with political issues, possibly terrorism. I needed to get in touch with London.

To reassure myself, I wandered near a bearded man wearing an old hat who sucked on a black cigarette from tobacco-stained fingers. When questioned he shrugged and said simply, "No English, me Russian." Now I was convinced there were political issues with these people and I moved to a Chinese lady who sat quietly holding some beads.

"Excuse me, ma'am, may I ask where you came from?" She looked at me blankly. I tried again. "Where is your home? Where you were born?"

She seemed to sense something and said politely, "English missionaries taught me a little when I was a girl in Nanking, long time before Japanese came and we ran."

This was hopeless. I decided to get some fresh air and a secure land line to call London and find someone at the Home Office who could advise me. A civil servant told me to leave it to the Detention Centre staff who would come down. Just then it started to rain and I sat in my car for a few moments. There was a tap on the window. One of the staff told me I was needed right away. When I reached the hall it was empty. I was furious. "Where the bloody hell are the illegals?" The Vicar came over.

"They've gone."

"Gone? How did they escape? What were my staff doing?"

"They didn't escape. They left."

"How?"

"I don't know. They simply got up and walked back to the coast, saying it was time to go."

"You mean some gang came to collect them?"

"No. They said they had to find refuge elsewhere."

"I need to go after them and round them up."

"You won't find them."

"What? They haven't been gone long."

"I saw them. They walked across the field that leads to the beach and before they reached the other side, they weren't there anymore."

Doubting the sanity of this clergywoman, my colleagues answered my furious enquiries by saying simply, "We didn't think it was right to stop them going back so we let them go."

"Back, back! Where to man?"

"Where they came from."

"And that is?"

"I couldn't say."

After a search confirmed the migrants had indeed flown, I returned, despondent to the church hall. The Vicar was waiting. "I knew you wouldn't find them."

I looked at her.

"They told me that they were all refugees. But they felt they didn't belong here. The Abyssinians fled the Italians and the German was escaping the Nazis. The Russian gentleman said he was afraid both of the Tsars and the revolutionaries. The Chinese lady was afraid for all her relatives left behind when Japan invaded. So they were all in flight, you see. They didn't know each other but they felt they should leave together."

When the detention centre staff arrived I said it was a false alarm. No one left to detain.

Old school ties

"Can I help you?"

"Yes, I think so."

"Oh, you're Mr Verdad? I do apologise, I was expecting a Spanish gentleman."

"No. My family connections were Spanish but I was born here."

"Oh, I see. Well, as you know this property needs some attention but its price reflects that and, well, frankly, it's in one of the best areas of the city. With a sympathetic updating you would see the value rise considerably."

"Yes. I like the area and it feels right, though I need to look around…"

"Of course. Let's go through to the kitchen. Just here."

"It looks on to the garden, good."

"Yes. And the garden is really quite a size for this part of the city. Not many have bigger plots, though again it has rather gone to seed but in essentials it remains a wonderful space. Now, next to this older scullery we have the passage to the dining room."

They stepped into the dining room.

"Do you know who lived here?"

"Well, the last owner let it out for a few years."

"No, I mean when we knew the area."

"I'm sorry, I don't really follow. The owners about fifteen years ago were connected in some way to the school I understand."

"Mr McVeigh."

"Yes…I think that was the name but it passed on to some relatives, a nephew I understand about fifteen years ago. Anyway, the ground floor has two reception rooms – one faces the road and the other is more private."

"I never knew the nephew."

"No…I have not exactly met him myself. His solicitor simply wants to expedite matters and get the thing sold. I forgot to ask if you need any financial advice because our office—"

"I have cash."

"Oh, good. Probably the safest bet for a sure sale. Surveys always bring up something and lenders don't always recognise the wood for the trees."

"Just as well, as you say, because I think the place has some dry rot."

"Really? That's the first I have heard. Are you sure? There's very little sign."

"You can always smell a bit of rot. Experience you know."

"Oh. I take it you're in that line of work then? Surveying I mean…"

"No. Just have a feel for things that haven't stood the test of time."

"Right. Well, you can see that the main stairway is pretty solid when we go up to the bedrooms. Of course, we have a downstairs toilet and sink but that needs updating as we'll see later."

The two men ascended the stairs. "It feels strange being here."

"Really? So you know the house then? I rather got the impression that you knew the area."

"I used to see this house when I came out of school."

"Oh, I see now. You were at the school. That makes sense."

"McVeigh was the Deputy Head."

"Yes, he was. Some time ago."

"And you were the head of Plunkett House."

"How did you know that?"

"You don't remember me."

"No, I don't."

"I remember you."

"Clearly. But I would have recalled that name."

"Verdad?"

"Yes."

"That's not my name."

"So, who are you, if I might ask? And what is this about?"

"It's about you and me."

"You being who, Mr…?"

"You think I'm buying this house?"

"No, I suppose not. You're not really a buyer, are you? What's your game?"

"I'm not buying because I already own this house."

"I don't believe you…"

"It doesn't matter what you believe, Devlin. It's beside the point."

"So what *is* the point, Mr Whoever you are?"

"Sangster. Remember now?"

"Wait…"

"Your little song for me,

"Sing a song of Sangster,
Nasty little gangster,
Needs to feel a hamster,
Biting through his Jamster."

"Yes. Sangster. I remember you now. I wouldn't have recognised you with that beard and without glasses."

"Last time you saw me…"

"You were expelled."

"Yes, I was. What for?"

"I can't remember."

"Yes, you can. Because you poured chemical acid all over my blazer and then reported me for tampering with dangerous acids in the chemistry lab. That was your *coup de grace* after years of bullying."

"Look, boys do stupid, even cruel things. We all did."

"Yes, we did. But you excelled in everything."

"So I was a bit of a sneak. What of it? It's long past. It's your problem if you haven't got over it."

"Oh, but I have. Or will have."

"What do you mean? Look, I've had enough of this stupid charade, Sangster."

"McVeigh. My name's McVeigh now. I changed my name. Bit of poetic justice."

"But that was the name of—"

"The deputy head who expelled me – on your say so. Yes."

"So why?"

"He made the house over to me. Before his death that is. You might wonder why because I had evidence against him. His hours of special treatment for some of the boys. You remember, Devlin. You knew about it. Even colluded with him as I recall."

"Nonsense. You can't dig any dirt up on me. And I'm going."

"No, you're not."

"My God, put that down. This is madness, man."

"Sit down."

"So what's your game? They're expecting me back at the office."

"Really? I booked the last slot of the day and I know you lock up."

"All right. What do you want?"

"I want what everyone wants, Devlin. A sense of retribution for wrongs suffered."

"Wrongs? Being expelled from school?"

"That was the beginning of a bad road for me. Depression, drugs, crime and finally daylight."

"What are you going to do?"

"That depends. Tonight, Mr McVeigh is going to disappear. Deep into his Spanish connections far from here. The house will be left derelict. The estate agent will never be found. Dissolved in acid. Stronger than the stuff you used on my blazer. But you do have a say in how you want to travel to your destination. Let's celebrate that, shall we?"

Friendly Confidences

"Why not?"

"Why not what?"

"Why don't you leave?"

"I like it here."

"It's bloody dangerous."

"For who?"

"Everyone. You in particular."

"Who says that?"

"People I talk to."

"Interesting friends."

"They're not friends."

"Confidences then. Like a confidential friend?"

"No."

"Maybe a priest? Your confessor."

"You'll want a priest if you go down this road."

"Okay. Know any good ones? I mean quality. For my send-off."

"I don't think you'll need an undertaker."

"No? You mean the priest will get me in a sack?"

"I mean your body will never be found."

"Cheap deal at the crematorium then? Just a few memories to burn?"

"You don't know what you're getting into. Don't be fucking stupid."

"What am I getting into? You know all about it. Tell me."

"I know that anyone who crosses these people – these animals I should say – won't be breathing for long."

"So what should I do? You're a friend. Advise me."

"You should leave this city. Tonight. Now. Just get out and don't look back."

"Okay, so I go. What happens then?"

"Whatever happens, happens. That won't concern you."

"What about you? You're supposed to be my friend. Why won't they come for you?"

"They might."

"So…why aren't you catching the midnight train, my good friend?"

"They don't think I can cause them the trouble that you've caused them."

"But I'll miss you."

"No, you won't."

"No. I won't. But you know what I will miss?"

"What?"

"The money. The money I won't get."

"What money are you talking about?"

"The money for not talking about the work I did for them. That money."

"Listen. I've spelled it out. You cannot fucking blackmail these people. They do the blackmailing. They don't pay blackmailers. They kill them."

"You know the thing that they hate even more than blackmailers?"

"Tell me."

"They hate informers worse than poison."

"Yeah. And if you try and inform on them, you'll be dead meat – chopped up for dog food."

"That's the only one of their rules I can really sign up to."

"Okay. So what? No one likes a grass."

"You still watch the football?"

"Yeah. What's that got to do with it?"

"On the telly the other week I saw this bloke who was full of the patter. Massive car, great watch, expensive haircut, you know the look."

"And?"

"He was a football agent. And he says, 'Everybody says they hate us. They call us parasites but everyone uses us. Openly or on the quiet. Everyone.' And he's right."

"What's your point?"

"Well, informers are just agents. They keep their ear to the ground and their eye on the money. They sell information and they sell people. The only thing they want to talk about is the price."

"Is this going anywhere?"

"The question is, am I going anywhere?"

"If you want to live long then the answer is 'yes'."

"So, anyway. I talk to this other friend of ours."

"Who?"

"Isn't important. The relevant point is what he told me."

"And."

"He was very cagey to start with. You know, distrustful. So I had to loosen him up. Relax him."

"You knocked him out?"

"No! Kept him fully alert right on his game. I had a little carrot and a very big stick."

"Look, time's getting short."

"That's just what I said to him. He didn't believe me because time was going very slowly for him. He wanted the conversation to end. Right quick."

"So. What did he say?"

"He told me that there was only one real grass on our street and he was very well known to me."

"You can't trust a punter you're beating to death…he'd say anything."

"Maybe. So, what did I do?"

"What?"

"I did what anyone would have done in my shoes. I checked his story."

"I've gotta move if we're not—"

"Make a move, friend, and it will definitely be your last. That's a promise."

"Look, man. I've come here to help you out, to make sure—"

"To make sure that I leave and that they have some idea where I'm going, right?"

"No! Don't tell me where you're going! Don't tell anyone. Just—"

"Shut up for a minute, will you? Because I need you to do something for me."

"I'd do anything for you but don't believe what that grass told you, just—"

"You're talking across me again."

"Sorry."

"Right. Now I need you to take me to them, lead me to them."

"I can't! I don't where they will be!"

"Yes, you do because you were to report to them after this little pep talk with me. Deny it and I'll break your arm."

"You're mad. They'll kill us both."

"Maybe. But I don't think so."

"Look, let's just get out of it together like the old days, you know. 'The Brothers' they called us."

"Yeah, they did. And if you don't do this. Tonight. You'll be my dead brother before morning."

"What do I have to do?"

"That's more like it. More like the old days. Brothers in arms. Well, here's the thing. To start with, we have to do a bit of shopping. I have a few tools. A single shooter. But we're gonna need a few more. Specialist stuff. Now, your axes and hammers, shotguns, they're way too crude for these blokes – the bosses. We need to treat them with a bit of respect. Don't you agree? For them I want a few precision tools. Need to do the work properly. That's what Churchill used to say, isn't it?"

"Churchill? What's he got to do with it?"

"Quite a lot. He said and I quote, 'Give us the tools and we'll finish the job!' He was talking about the Nazis but you get my point?"

"Yes."

"Good man. Who knows? You might even see tomorrow night after all. Let's do the shopping. You know all about that. Don't you?"

Elephants

"The conference is bloody boring."

"I heard one good paper yesterday."

"Are you staying in the halls of residence?"

"They're not my favourite place."

"I had forgotten you were resident here."

"Had you forgotten?"

"Well, not that you were here. What was it – two years?"

"Yes. The job contract was very limited."

"Well, they are bloody tight with the college money at the best of times – it's not that easy now."

"Really? Some people were luckier. Maybe that hasn't changed."

"You mean Trevor? Well, he had a fairly heavyweight patron."

"And I just had you."

"Look, Andrew. I know you got a rough deal and if I could have done more."

"Oh, don't worry, I know you did your best."

"Thanks. I felt bloody awful about the way you were pushed out."

"Why was that?"

"What? Well, I don't know all the machinations that went on but when it came down to it, we just didn't have enough guns."

"No, I meant why did you feel awful about it?"

"It's obvious, isn't it? You were a friend of mine, my protégé if you like and it was as much a slap in the face for me as for you."

"Not quite as hard a slap for you though, Jonathan."

"No, you're right. You came off worse. No job and all that. We all said it was really bad – what happened."

"Well, it was the right thing in the long-run I think. Breaking away from this place with its high table snobbery and terrible food."

"We had to sack the cook and that porter who got drunk and fell off his perch in the chapel!"

"High jinks. So was I part of a general clear out? Or just booted out alone?"

"Look, I know we lost touch after you…well, after you left. I just didn't know what to say. I know it was rough out there."

"You mean 'out there' in the real world? Well, it was a bit. After all the plans we had, I was a bit lost. Vulnerable."

"Yes. I heard."

"What did you hear?"

"Just that you had to take some time out. Weren't too bright for a while."

"Very English way of referring to three or four years of clinical depression."

"All credit to you that you turned things around. Came back into the game. Everyone said it took guts to do that. Trevor particularly."

"Trevor? Didn't know he was big on guts."

"Look. We didn't know what to do for the best. When you became – well, isolated like that."

"I'd like to set the record straight on that one. Just for old time's sake."

"Go ahead. You've got every right to."

"You could say that my 'crisis', if that's what it was, came before the sacking. When I found out about Sophie quite a bit before everything else."

"You found out? What?"

"That you had been sleeping with her. When we finally broke up she said I should cut my ties with you for everyone's sake."

"She told you? God. You must have thought I was a total shit. All I can say is she made the move. I was never that involved."

"I might say that confession of – what? Indifference? That puts the icing on the cake – or the turd, whichever you prefer. Well, we were both shits because I wasn't heartbroken that we finished. I wasn't even deeply offended that you had been fucking her on the side. Your womanising was always part of you. I knew that. I didn't really take it personally."

"Well, I am really sorry and it's big of you not to despise me."

"Don't misunderstand me. I didn't say I don't despise you."

"Okay. Can't complain if you feel that way."

"No, it's only that I never felt your sexual betrayal was born out of any animosity. To me – personally."

"You're right that I didn't intend you to know – or get hurt."

"I was almost as heartless a bastard in my 'romantic' relationships as you were. In those days women were somehow unimportant compared to 'The Work'."

"We had ambitions."

"Strange how we find out what's really important and who we really love. That's what I finally worked out."

"You met someone else?"

"No. I met someone I thought I had known a long time. I met you."

"I can't keep on apologising."

"You can't apologise. I know. The sacking and Sophie, they were just the luck of the draw. Lots of people were struggling with work and partners in those years. Bloody difficult time."

"I did ask Trevor how you were getting on and if we could do something for you."

"Well, Trevor did help out in a way. Unintended consequences and all that."

"Oh, I didn't know he kept in touch."

"Not directly, you understand. But he let slip that the journal business all began with you, not him, not the editors."

"The journal business?"

"You didn't think I found out? That you said my submission, based on our work, was plagiarising yours?"

"I never put it like that."

"I read your report."

"Well, you could have asked me."

"You bloody liar. I sent you a draft almost a year before. You said nothing but 'good luck with finding a home for it.'"

"So what do you want me to say?"

"Nothing. It was that which sent me down into that pit for a while. But not some bloody lost publication."

"I thought you were pulling a fast one."

"No, you didn't. You wanted me dead, professionally. Then you could build on the work alone. But so what? The discovery I made in that shitstorm was that I had loved you utterly with my soul. When you destroyed that love, you nearly destroyed my mind. But then I saw you for the first time and I was free of you and everyone else. I knew that I could never again feel that for another human being ever, so I owe you one."

Dress Sense

My mother liked a well-dressed man. "Well turned out" is how she would put it, measuring out some well-tailored guy with those keen eyes. I wonder if she thinks I've turned out well. Mother knew her clothes. No question, travelling miles to get a silk scarf that would match her elegant 'French green' cocktail dress. Fussy perhaps but she had to be professional. She was still working in the escort business well into her forties. High class ass my old mum, though she would hate the Americanism. Last I heard she was part of a comfortable *menage a trois* on the Costa Brava, yacht trips included.

Me? Never shared her passion for clothes but I do have a favourite suit. Take it everywhere with me and it has a name: Winston. You can just see the faded brand mark on the neck. Winston's been with me on my best days and he's saved my life more than once. He's a wet one and in quite good nick. We go scuba diving or bottle diving whenever and wherever the water's warm enough. Calling him a lifesaver doesn't just mean keeping hypothermia at bay or protecting skin against all the scrapes you get on coral reef dives. Winston's given me insights. Knowledge that soaks in when you've got time to think. And that's the most important thing I need in my line of work. Down there you find quiet and a kind of peace, a serenity that's hard to find above the water line. Take an example. When I was diving off Japan, mainly around Okinawa, I learned a lot about the nice things and nasty things you uncover in the open sea. Puffer Fish for example. Kills fifty people a year in Japan. Not under the water but in their own kitchens. Talking to a knowledgeable guy about these things, a marine biologist in Korea, we got on to chatting about the sea urchins you meet on a dive. He reckoned the scratch of a Flower Urchin produces enough Peditoxin and Contractin to send you into anaphylactic shock before you know what's hit you. He said that toxic 'TTX' carried by the Blue Ringed Octopus was more lethal again. No antidote. This stuff is the fastest road to a heart attack you'll ever take.

You're wondering why I'm drifting around with my old sea-stories and not getting to the point. All in good time. In my trade I'm called a Looper. That's the bloke who loops together all the little bits of information you need to make a story that people want to hear. You might say I'm a string theorist. They're your anglers who accept the chaos of life, of existence even, and see the point of it all. I was given this assignment of stringing together some very bright but difficult young guys in Japan. They were nicking video game designs, software and all, and making their own games – a lot slicker than the originals. They caused chaos because they didn't sell the ideas to the owners but passed them to a distributor who made millions for them. They were still working and my job was to find the real genius in their group. Took a bit of work to arrange for him to be served bad Puffer Fish at his favourite restaurant, particularly when he didn't order that dish. The boy-wonder was out of action for a few months and never quite the same again. Job done. And with that contract fee I had enough time to do a bit more scuba diving.

Makes my point that know-how is everything. Where's this going I hear both you and me asking: to Gravesend actually. Job there was just to find out what container ship was bringing in the goods that these mega people-traffickers and merchandise smugglers had commissioned. An Albanian and two Lebanese brothers. So this bloke I don't really know sends over a drink to me in this pub with this little message 'Good diving'. Did I know him from scuba? As I nod to him I felt this little prick in my thigh. Slim young Asian woman was disappearing out of the side door. I look straight at my drink and my benefactor who makes to go, pronto. I know it's an emergency job. Could feel my leg going numb. Now or never. I race after this bloke, sweating in no time and he's running like his life depended on it. Too true. I bring him down on the old railway tracks.

"What is it?" I ask.

"Just paid to buy you a drink, mate!"

"Drugged was it? What was the needle?"

"Don't know, honest. Toxin they said."

Dead loss. No real knowledge. So I smashed him in the windpipe and that was that. Job done.

Got to a corner and taxi to the nearest hospital almost unconscious when I told them probably marine toxin could be Peditoxin. After that a kind of coma for more than a month.

They paid me only after I found the Flower Urchin who stabbed me in the pub. Had to explain to her about the Blue Octopus toxin in my hypodermic before she gave me what she knew. How they had turned me over; someone talked to the Lebos. A couple of weeks back at the boxing gym and it was time for some R&R. Diving off Sharm El-Sheikh and then to Beirut to look up my new friends. Tracked down the older Lebo to a swimming pool in Mimas, not far from the Maronite College. Toxins might be good enough for the younger brother but for this solid chunky guy I decided on something a bit melodramatic. Not like me but Winston convinced me. Used the spear-gun. Impossible to extract once in. Used it lots of times on the coral reefs. Never on a fish as fat as this one.

Wedding Weeds

It was her wedding day and she had to make preparations. Some people had never believed it would happen. She could tell from their eyes that they still thought she might be jilted at the altar rail. But she knew her Harold far better than they did. She held not a scintilla of doubt that he would carry her back home in her beautiful dress. Before she could lay out her pearly white trousseau on the bed, she felt the first unmistakable tremors of an earthquake. She usually knew when one was going to strike but her mind had been so absorbed in anticipating the wedding day that she was taken completely off guard. The floor of her room began to shake and the walls tilted at an impossible angle. Inside she could feel the dull relentless rumbling of the volcano that swept everything around her into unreal distorted dimensions. Bells were ringing, voices calling and sirens sounded as the morning light glittered on her wall mirror. It shivered like the water on the boating lake but didn't break. That meant her luck would hold. If only she could hang on she would still see her hopes fulfilled. As she fell on to the bed her hands clapped together in senseless applause and her legs shook like corn stalks in a storm.

She felt a hand reach hers and she grasped it as tightly as she held Harold's when she stepped from that wobbly rowing boat on the lake. *Terra firma*. The tremors began to subside. She recognised the hand as one of the young women who helped out in her hotel.

"Take this, Mrs Arnott and you'll soon feel better."

She was offering her some kind of medicine in a small pink cup. Why did she think she was already married? Had rumours been flying that she and Harold had made their vows in a secret ceremony as they had always said they would? Something was wrong. To be polite she took the drink and asked for a cup of breakfast tea. Sometimes they brought Lady Grey and the scent of it made her feel faint. Teas don't need fancy names do they? They all come from what we used to call Ceylon. What's it called now? Surinam? Something like that.

Her thoughts returned to her wedding dress. She wondered if she should wear her mother's pearls with it. Firstly, she needed to decide on her hair. It had always been a lovely shade of auburn. Harold said it was her hair that first caught his eye in that dance when he was still in uniform. When was that? It couldn't have been that long ago. Time could get so mashed up in here like the corned beef hash her mother made when the rationing went on longer than expected. Was that last year or a year before that? Didn't matter. What mattered was her big day.

People were always confusing dates and losing her photographs that they should have kept. Like that man who came to see her a week or two ago...or whenever. What did he say? Oh yes, he said he was her son and that he had brought his Moira to see her. I told him it was nonsense. Out of wedlock? Never. He did look a bit like Harold. Must have been that younger brother no one talked about. I had to tell him, "This is not, Moira. Moira was such a lovely slim girl. This woman's fat. Who is she?" Anyway, she never came again. He said I had upset her. Well, I had to say people should watch what they eat. I could still fit in my wedding dress and that was…what am I thinking? I'm going to find the dress now and meet Harold. He used to sing *On a bicycle made for two* and we laughed. I'm sure he'll have a car at the church. It was just our little joke.

Her tea arrived but she refused a biscuit. Need dry lips for the lipstick and everything had to be just so on this day of all days. She imagined the vicar asking her, "And do you, Delia, take Herbert to be your lawful wedded husband?"

She would flinch a little before offering the "Yes." She never liked 'Herbert' and it was to please her that he changed it to Harold. Everyone now called him Harold or Harry. She loved Laurence Olivier as Henry V and everyone called him Harry, "For England, Harry and Saint George!" A good English name that. Half her neighbours seem to come from Surinam these days. Even these hotel girls.

Finally, the maids of honour arrived to dress her. They couldn't find the wedding dress. After a bit of a tizzy she accepted the nice light blue dress that they brought out. She insisted on a sprig of flowers and her hat, of course. One of them said, "Quite right, Mrs Arnott. I'm sure he would want you dressed in something bright and beautiful." She wasn't the full shilling that one but she had the right idea about colours. Grant her that. Delia walked slowly with good posture to the wedding car. That man was there again, standing at the car door like a chauffeur but without his Moira.

He sat with her so he must be a relative. Was he giving her away? Perhaps a black sheep of Harold's family or a friend he kept quiet? No secrets when we're married. As the car approached the church there was one long black one with lots of flowers. An odd shape and the men around looked like butlers from some posh mansion. Perhaps Lady Grey had turned up? She would tell her soon-to-be husband that joke. The moment had finally arrived: it was 'Showtime' as Harold would tell her. They both had to put their best foot forward. She wasn't going to let him down. Not today of all days.

Section 6:
Passions Uncovered

A Taste of Tango

The hall was empty but not quiet. There was the sound of Carlos Gardel singing as though it was 1933 and the sun was shining on the pampas far beyond Buenos Aires. It was not. The sun had gone down on Dudley the day before yesterday and had not reappeared through the autumn clouds since. Only the faint breeze murmured in agreement with Gardel that this was to be a grey afternoon and evening. Hector had left the tape running for a good reason; it was his birthday and he wanted everyone to realise he was having a wonderful time even if he could not be present to celebrate it. He was recovering from the break-up of his relationship with Emily and was in his flat over the hall, nursing an inclination to get drunk on cheap wine.

Last year, Emily had gone to live in Buenos Aires for six months and met a teacher from Barcelona. She moved to Catalonia to be 'close to tango', though it was also closer to Eduardo. On discovering he had not one but two additional girlfriends with whom he spent his leisure hours, Emily tried hard but failed to persuade him that he was in crisis about his mother and so she signed herself into a therapy clinic. There she fell deeply in love with her neuroses and decided they should accompany her on her epic journey to find deeper tango. She no longer hoped to find deeper *milongueros* but they must remain in the picture if she was to retain an authentic feel of the dark beauty of tango. Emily considered changing her name to Malena in honour of her heroine, the subject of a famous tango song but decided she must find herself first. She kept an exhaustive diary of her tango experiences and the moods that they engendered in her soul. Her therapist advised giving up the dance for a little while at least clearly failing to understand what dancers go through. She gave up the talking cures and spent the money on classes in ladies' technique. Her *voleos* became the talk of the women's rows in the *milongas* she frequented.

Then the money ran out. Her tenant back in the English midlands left her small house to get married and her brother asked for a loan to be repaid. She had to return. Spanish was no longer heard on the streets she walked but a form of Brummie English together with ethnic pronunciations of the same. To console herself she listened endlessly to different versions of 'Malena', sung in a soulful way with all the suffering that she felt she needed to express. Then something happened. Ricardo arrived from Harrogate. He was an unemployed Argentinian who had been living with a Welsh girlfriend in this Yorkshire town populated by conservative retirees and trying to interest them in the dark embrace of tango. Ricardo ran up against the popularity of sequence dancing and the arrival of Stetson-wearing line dancers. He was not helped by his uncertain grasp of English vowels and the strange manners of these provincial people who had money but limited understanding of how to spend it or enjoy doing so. Fatigued, he broke with his girlfriend, pawned his uncle's bandoneon and moved to the midlands. Emily saw him dancing in a milonga arranged in a working man's club and was entranced. He was not exactly handsome, having the long-faced looks of a lesser Conquistador from the time of Pizzaro rather than the cool beauty of the Genoese who came to Argentina by the boatload in the 1890s. But he had something and she wanted that thing.

They talked. They had sex twice. It wasn't tango but it was good. Sufficient. Then Ricardo had the idea of a local tango 'encuentro' with a kind of 'mini-mundial', which is Birmingham English meant a *milonga* that last two days and some kind of dance-off where the most talented or popular couple would be considered the stars of the event. It seemed a good idea and Emily persuaded two or three enthusiasts to help out and several people were keen to play the tango tracks over the two days. The first day was almost perfect as people greeted her as the companion of the dazzling Ricardo. She danced not much but very well and gathered the confidence of the room around her. Then she heard the gossip. Unintentionally. Someone who was not a regular and who drank two glasses of Malbec wine when she should have stopped at one, confided in a whisper, "And I hear he the quite the romantic lover! Argentinian men are all supposed to be the same. Someone told me he has at least three women at this *encuentro* and more are queuing up." She giggled and headed off for more wine before it disappeared.

Emily was not shocked. She knew what tango teachers were like – or rather what many Argentinian men and women could be like when they were given opportunities. What was shocking was that the news suddenly made her think of her father. He had been seriously ill for weeks and her brother said he wanted to see her. She had had so little to do with her unsympathetic parents for years and took little notice of the news. She did not believe in premonition so when her cell phone rang the next day and her brother told her that their father was now gravely ill, she knew it was the end. As she left the hall, Ricardo caught her arm and asked if she would be one of the judges to decide the best couple at their event. "Emily. It has been a success. Thank you." She didn't answer but turned towards the door. On an impulse she dropped her new tango shoes into the large black bin that stood nearby. Above it was the notice 'Only for rubbish that cannot be recycled'.

Found in Translation

When Josephine met Juan Manuel she knew that her prayers had been answered. He was not so good looking that she would be worried every night she did not see him. He was not so intelligent that she would feel outclassed in every conversation about music or Marquez, lost in a hundred years of solitude or plague by an outbreak of cholera in their romance. Yes, he was very popular and that was a potential drawback but he was most popular with his football friends and she knew that if she never attempted to throw a party or expect a date or even a kiss when Boca Juniors were playing then she would never be in serious jeopardy. After so many broken affairs with Argentine men who never promised anything but their hearts and never delivered anything except their bodies, minus the heart, she thought that she had discovered gold in the streets of Buenos Aires. Juan Manuel agreed that she was lucky because he was not interested in other women and was happy to go along with her ideas of domestic bliss even if he didn't much care for her taste in wallpaper or her refusal to wear boots in bed. But he reflected that life could not be perfect all the time and he still had his nights on his own and with friends that she understood belonged to him and not to her and nor were these excursions coupled to their love train.

Juan Manuel was more complex than he pretended. He lived happily within a relationship but he preserved a rich interior life that was decorated by himself and was full of unmade beds and uncluttered by promises of lifelong fidelity. Freedom was necessary to him, just as the company of an attractive woman was an essential part of his constitution. Josephine not only gave him moments of satisfaction and stability but did not try to possess him completely as so many Argentine women did. True, she did not really understand Argentine culture for she had only lived there for seven years and that was not a sufficient time to encounter all the crazy dimensions of this city let alone the surrealist contrasts of the regions of Argentina. He knew. His father's family was from the north, beyond Salta and his mother's mother had come from Patagonia where she had worked for German people on a farm. She called them German though they were descendants of people who came to Argentina in the 1920s and refused to mix with the later German immigrants with their shady National Socialist connections. To Beatrice they were all Germans. But Josephine was from France and had the beauty and the temperament of someone who listens to opera with half closed eyes and drinks in the perfume of Paris with the relaxed relish of a true sophisticate. Juan Manuel thought that he might look like that when he tasted the fresh saltiness of victory when his beloved footballers closed down their opponents with a brilliant goal. He had to acknowledge that the hysterical release of joy felt on the steps of La Boca Stadium was closer to frantic ecstasy than the cool civilisation that Josephine might experience. But who knows? Did the language of either country capture the whispers of the soul on such nights? Probably not.

His moments of ecstasy were not confined to raucous triumph in the fleeting glory of the football field. This was where they discovered that Destiny is real. Each had agreed that 'character is destiny' and that if they both wanted something it would happen. They had been intensely loyal for almost five months and their love affair was as secure as anything could be in a country that swung from economic crisis to emotional disorder with the confident muscularity of a trapeze artist. Then disaster struck in a form that was completely unanticipated. Juan Manuel spent his free nights in areas of the city that she never went. In particular he liked to mingle on the Avenida Libertador where you could see the expensive cars race by and the beautiful bodies poured out from expensive private gymnasia as the aeroplanes swam around overhead from Jorge Newbery airport. Josephine spent these nights with her girlfriends, usually in San Christobel or San Telmo where she danced both tango and folklore. Juan Manuel hated tango as much as he loved football, though in other respects he had the soul of an artist. On this night she met Chiara who was having an engagement party with her female friends because Geronimo, her lover, refused to consider an engagement official until he had talked to his mother and this he was afraid to do. They had been engaged three weeks and Chiara decided enough was enough. Not only did she arrange for a male stripper but she ordered a limousine to transport her friends to the private club where said stripper would perform in style. Josephine explained this to Juan Manuel who showed no interest but said 'Bravo' and read a football programme from a game he had unusually and very sadly missed.

The night was a success though the stripper was a disappointment with a flaccid penis that displayed little excitement throughout the whole performance. However, the champagne dulled the edge of the deflation the women understandably felt. As they crowded into their limousine intent on finding a good milonga where they might express their unrequited passion on some likely suspects, the stripper rushed out and asked them for a ride. This request was capable of different interpretations but he made it clear he only needed a taxi a few blocks to see a friend. Their sleek car stretched like a panther and sped them down the Avenida Libertador and slowed as the stripper (he was called Fernando but had a stage name they couldn't understand), called 'Here! Here!' The women pushed down the windows of the car as Fernando exited and saw him walk steadily towards an exotic woman in a tight dress and narrow hips. She was heavily but tastefully made up and turned to the arrival and kissed him full on the lips. The passengers were slightly affronted by Fernando's evident readiness to find arousal with this stranger after they had failed to draw his amorous intentions but Chiara shrugged and Josephine continued to watch as they prepared to drive on. She might never have understood her strange feeling of interest in the *femme fatale* if she had not spoken to Fernando. In a husky voice she rasped, "We'll meet later. A man in a Mercedes has passed twice. He'll be back for sure. Go on! See you at Gero's place." She blew him a kiss and then caught Josephine's eye. They both knew. Juan Manuel's voice was unmistakeable even if his protruding breasts were not.

In that moment of translation their unspoken conversation flashed before them like the water on a sunlit stream when a fish suddenly leaps up and is held for a moment in the unreal glory of full exposure. And then falls back to its natural element. Each considered whether it was possible to continue a relationship where this private world had invaded their own fixed terrain. Could he bring this trans-sexual desire into the full flower of their intimacy and yet sustain its secret bloom as something preciously personal and even furtive in its excitement? Josephine was so unwilling to lose in a reckless moment of chance all that she had longed for and yet each of them recognised that it was simply impossible to translate this private language of erotic yearning and sexual transactions into the very different tongue of their agreed romance. For all of their apparent liberalism in matters of the heart, they both held on to deeply convention ideals of romantic attachment. It was a loyalty to all of the cherished illusions that had entranced lovers for generations. Grandmothers from Salta or Patagonia as well as Paris. There was a brief, almost invisible moment of tender sadness as Josephine wound up the window and Juan Manuel gave a very faint half smile. As Chiara's magical coach of dreams pulled away, a silver Mercedes was slowing to a stop alongside her former lover.

Ernesto Reborn

Those in the know will tell you that if you want to be a tango dancer, a real *milonguero*, then you have to learn how to move. They can tell how long you've been dancing tango and if you'll ever dance well simply by watching you walk. Some people look at financial newspapers and they see stocks and shares, bonds and trusts, moving before their eyes. Same with tango. You need to see the value in between the lines, potential spaces and how you exploit them. The big unknown, the black box of this dance, is that after spending years trying to get your feet in the right places, you might still not be the dancer you dreamed about. The missing ingredient is probably style. This doesn't mean flashy. It's better if you're not but it has to be something that belongs to you. Style has to be worn like a suit. It has to look comfortable, even natural on you, fitting as closely as your own skin. Some people never know what's missing and others try to borrow a style. But you can't drag it off someone else. His suit, his skin wouldn't fit you. You have to make it yourself. For you.

If you worry about these things, then tango has taken you over – that's what I learned when I tried to figure out what happened to Ernie Waters. We all knew him when worked in life insurance in Doncaster before he moved one step further and sold funeral insurance – persuading people how important it was to pay for their own death and not leave it to someone else to foot the bill. Ernie was very good at it and had a gift for pushing expensive tombstones, so the funeral directors always made sure he had a happy Christmas. One day he saw the writing on his own headstone, as it were, and decided to retire while he could still stand. He took up dancing. Did quite a bit of old-time and sequence dancing before he discovered tango. It happened one night in a club in Rotherham. An old guy who had served as a ship's engineer and did regular runs to South America brought tango back with him from Buenos Aires. He taught a little class in Rotherham and another in Barnsley. Eric's best dancing years were far behind him but he could still find his way around the floor with something like style.

Ernie was mesmerised. Tango took him to a place completely different from the stale repetition of sequence dancing. He was determined to learn and spent the next year looking for his tango feet. Without a lot of prompting from Eric he brought different women to learn with him and he helped to organise the little *milongas* that were held on the outskirts of northern towns. Their names guaranteed that the two men would become known as 'the tango comedians' after their more famous Morecambe namesakes but Ernie was soon to break away from Eric and began travelling farther afield to dance tango in Sheffield, Nottingham and even Manchester. It was in Oldham that Ernie met the woman who changed his life. Not in any romantic way. Ernie had never felt the same since his prostate operation, which had followed a hernia he developed when helping stone masons load headstones he had commissioned. In any case, Doreen was too garrulous for him to bear. He hardly heard his favourite tango tracks undisturbed if he sat near her. The great value she brought was in her recollections of Argentina. Eric had never shared many memories of his days below the equator but Doreen was only too happy to spread her reminiscences around the table like Tarot cards.

Within weeks he was converted to the Argentine pilgrimage. He must go. The flight was booked, a likely tango landlady was recommended by Doreen and he carefully folded hundreds of American dollars in the money-belt he fastened next to his underpants. The exhausting flight was concluded and airport queues navigated before catching a taxi to the ciudad. He stayed only three weeks but returned a changed man. Before his trip he thought Frank Sinatra was the summit of style. In Argentina he learned about Carlos Gardel, who sang in Spanish and was every inch a movie star singer when Sinatra was still a kid. Ernie's head had been truly turned and he now faced west whenever he could. He bought tango music by the armful and tried to learn some Spanish. This was not a great success but he was not discouraged. Soon he began to teach individuals tango. Not as Ernie former death salesman but Ernesto the *tanguero*. Former friends found it faintly bewildering if not ridiculous. Ernesto was unconcerned as he connected with as many experienced tango *companeros* as he could find. On his second trip to Buenos Aires he stayed four weeks and was measured for a suit. When he approached the dance floor one evening, in his cautious, padding step, he was ironically hailed by one native lady as 'El Leopardo'. He eagerly accepted the title, minus the disparaging tone, retelling the story as a moment of enviable triumph.

In truth, Ernie never became a superlative dancer though like Walter Mitty, he never surrendered his glorious dreams as he continued to visit his adopted city every year. He impressed people who knew little of the complex, often superficial and extravagant romance of the famous tango capital. Rioplatense Spanish remained beyond his linguistic reach just as the finer points of Argentine technique eluded him. But the *portenos* or city natives acquired a genuine affection for this strange *extranjero* or gringo because his passion for tango was so transparent and sincere. El Leopardo also acquired a style of dancing peculiar to himself which was never elegant and rarely resembled a stalking leopard but acquired a kind of fluid musicality that even the seasoned *tangueros* could glance at without feeling amused or offended.

Swimsuits

Her mother called to her through the bathroom door. It was unusual for her to be late for breakfast, for school, for anything. Her blazer was carefully pressed every week and she drew only quiet praise from teachers who marked her as an 'asset' to the academy, already projected as a star performer in examinations that lay two years away. She attracted girls with similar ambitions, no longer childish but clinging to their childhood toys, the remnants of a disappearing age. The boys somehow understood the virginal purity of such girls and were careful not to tease them roughly, the shyer ones were abashed by her serene prettiness.

Miss Carmichael insisted on being called 'Miss' and protected her bright girls, nurturing them as an intellectual stage mother, easing them gently towards stellar performance. She noticed Sarah's ability in the history project, reconstructing the last days of Pompeii, though her descriptions of civic life were more innocent than demure. In recent days she had seemed distracted, though she had shone unexpectedly in reading out the poetry of Philip Larkin and shocked her teacher's prim deference in describing James Joyce's stories as 'vulgar'. Allowances must be made for genius, she had written at the foot of Sarah's last essay. Even so, she could see genuine talent in this girl gliding gracefully towards intellectual womanhood.

The subject herself remained blithely unconscious of the vivid expectations aroused in the staff room, though she responded to her mother's familiar urging, "Handsome looks should make for handsome efforts." In recent days she had found it uncommonly difficult to concentrate on her studies, unaware of any particular reason for an inclination to drift away from the page and towards the trees that swayed like bodies along the near horizon. In school games she remained energetic though the hearty cheering of the other girls left her unexcited. She loved swimming more because it gave her a feeling of solitary freedom as she dived under the chlorinated water and gazed at the thrashing legs around her. Her imagination suddenly burst into a fantasy that she was a mermaid exploring unknown corals from which she would make herself – or someone else – a fabulous crown. These images surprised her, on sober reflection, for she rarely indulged in daydreams and had little interest in the growing passion for boy-singer fantasies among her school year.

This day she was given an hour of independent study in the library before her Spanish class and prepared dutifully rather than hopefully for the geography fieldwork that was arranged for next week. Sorting her Spanish reading she noticed, as if for the first time, the lean figure of the Matador in the text book, straining his leg muscles as he awaited the arrival of a huge bull. Somewhere in her memory she recollected the myth of a Minotaur inside a shadowy maze, combining in his body the dark power of the bull and the driven desires of manhood. Vaguely, she understood the appeal of such images for people who had lived with bulls for thousands of years.

A distant bell shook her mind from these thoughts and allowed her to focus on her vocabulary, pinning down slippery verbs that evaded regular conjugation. Spanish class proved uneventful and she met with two friends for an early lunch of sandwiches before leaving them to collect her laptop from her locker. On reaching the locker she felt a sudden impulse to use the swimming pool before classes recommenced and the pool would be occupied by the polo training team. This was uncharacteristic of her. Her day was usually planned in early morning and suffered few intrusions from passing fancies. *Maybe it's a good thing – that I'm changing my routine*, she thought as she booked out a large swimming towel.

That was the last coherent reflection she could afterwards recall. Walking towards the girl's entrance to the changing rooms she stopped suddenly, involuntarily. Her gaze had been captured by the sight of a wall seen through the slight opening of the boy's changing room. There hung three or four swimming costumes, dripping wet from recent use and glistening in the noon sunlight. They seemed to be red or black or both and they swayed without effort or breeze as they clung, like heavy birds, to their hooks. She heard a buzzing in her ears as her mind crowded with images, pressing forward as she struggled to push them back, striving to regain poise and clarity.

The torrent assailing her was too powerful. Images she had ignored, visions she had suppressed, sounds she had silenced, now cascaded like a warm, washing rain on a sultry terrain far away from school. Her nostrils tingled as she closed her eyes and recalled the Matador, now held on the shoulders of a Minotaur who led her towards the forbidden murals of erotic love on the walls of Pompeii, the plaster imprinted with the sexual ecstasy of a thousand years. Her breath shortened and her breasts rose as she pushed away James Joyce only to hear Philip Larkin calling to her of girls – like her – on railway platforms at *Whitsun Weddings*, gazing at departing brides from within a trance that beheld a 'religious wounding'. She flinched, feeling the coals of the Pompeii volcano explode and fall irresistibly on her burning skin, her body was flushed with ardent, inexplicable, sensuality as she accepted the invitation to desire.

As the crisis passed, rinsing through her body, she breathed again, opening her eyes. She was alone. Her first thought was to find relief in discovering that no other had witnessed her surrender to passion. Was this a momentary confusion, an abandonment of a chaste life readily reclaimed? Reverting to a studious, exemplary existence upon which adult expectations had been quietly but irresistibly placed? Opening her eyes widely now she knew the moment had belonged to her. This was the first sighting of a coming womanhood, waving to her from the slopes of a warm, foreign mountainside.

Lone Ranger

"Want to tell me what you were doing outside the cinema?"

"Whishhhhooooooo. That wind's comin' up the valley."

"What's blowing the wind, Stephen? That's your name, isn't it?"

"Sounds like the steers are gettin' kinda restless."

"Stephen? Your second name?"

"Most folks call me 'Paso'."

"'Paso'? Is that your family name?"

"Short for El Paso. Place I used to ride through."

"The arresting officer says you were causing a bit of a disturbance in the High Street outside the cinema. What was that about?"

"A man's gotta tell the truth."

"About what?"

"That moving picture they were showin' folks. It was all wrong."

"Tell me. Are you local Stephen?"

"It's Paso."

"Are you from around here, Paso?"

"Just passin' through."

"Well, look. I'm a probation officer, right?"

"You mean a sort of deputy?"

"I was about to go off my shift here when you were brought in. That's why I'm asking you these questions."

"When's the judge coming to town?"

"Let me ask you, Ste – Paso, where are you living? You're not a juvenile. We'd like to release you but we need to know you'll be okay."

"I'll be fine, deputy. They were just some saddle tramps hangin' around my chuck fire."

"So, you're living rough – sleeping rough somewhere?"

"I've been roughin' most of my life. Driftin' kinda suits me. Just the stars for a roof. Open prairie. Wooooooo…breeze getting' up. Need to be movin' on now, friend."

"Right. There is a shelter across the shopping precinct – just a few blocks from here. We could ring them.

"Well, last time I heard them church bells ringin' I knew that Mateo had hit town."

"Mateo?"

"Mateo is not the kinda dude you wanna meet on a rainy nite comin' outta the saloon. He'd just as soon knife you as spit at you."

"Well, life on the streets can be dangerous."

"Life on any street, any town, can be dangerous if the man facin' you is mean enough."

"True. But you don't have to live that way. There's help for people with, erm, problems adapting. Not mental health services, just people offering to listen."

"Just run that by me again? What do they wanna listen to exactly? I have a guitar but never played for anyone but my horse."

"What I'm trying to say is we would like to know more about you. Your history. Perhaps we could contact someone who could help you. Family or friends."

"Never been big on family after Ma passed. Pa kinda took up with drinkin' and a bit of whorin' and such. That was when my brother and I moved on."

"You have a brother? Can we get in touch with him? Do you have a telephone number – or an address for him?"

"Lost touch with Aaron after that trouble in Abilene – I don't say he was wrong doin' what he done. But I don't hold with beatin' a man with a fence post over a card game."

"I see. Bit of a dead end then?"

"You could say that. Aaron might be still breathin' for all I know."

"I really have to go off soon and I would like to decide, with you, what your immediate plans are and what help you need."

"That's mighty kind of you fella but to tell you straight, I gotta be headin' out. Maybe stay in the stables tonight and hit the trail early in the mornin'."

"I have to write some kind of report. Won't take long. Just your name and maybe where we might contact you – social services could offer you help."

"Mighty obliged but I'm fine. Sounds like you folks are kinda Churchy people around here. With your goodwill an' all. But there is one thing you could maybe do?"

173

"Yes? What's that?"

"Well, there's this fella I crossed today who seemed just plain bad. He's sellin' this bad stuff – worse than an old snake oil hustler – to kids just around the block. Bad dude. When I mosied past him he swore, said if I didn't get out of his way, he'd put me in the ground. But it didn't sit right with me, what he was doin'."

"He was what, a drug dealer? They're dangerous people."

"Yeah. That's what I figured."

"You should keep well away."

"That's what folks say when they know there's a problem but they're not aiming to fix it – anytime soon anyways."

"There are laws but—"

"Reckon the marshall is two days ride from here. This is somethin' I just gotta deal with before hittin' the trail. I just wouldn't rest easy knowin' that low-life swindler was out there killin' folks."

"What do you plan to do?"

"Well, I'll tell ya. I've never been quick to anger. Never had much use for handguns and such like but my daddy taught me how to break in a horse and how to deal with a roughneck. No cow puncher ever put me down in a fair fight."

"Don't expect these dealers to fight fair. Probably have knives or worse."

"That's what I figured, so I'm fixing to get prepared 'fore we dance. Toe to toe like."

"You really want to take these risks, er, Paso?"

"Sure thing, Mister. One thing this body knows somethin' about is them risks."

"Well, I'm going to ask the desk sergeant – I mean the sheriff – to give you some cash out the desk to cover a night's board. At 'the stables' if you like. Then its farewell, I guess."

"Mighty obliged. If you don't hear nothin' of this dealer fella, just pat yourself on the back for helpin' to fight the good fight, pardner."

"I'll do that, Paso."

"Okay. Sounds like it's high time for me to be meetin' that hombre with the bad hat."

"Good luck, Paso."

"You too, amigo."

"Adios."

"Adios my friend. Y'know, you're a kinda stand-up guy. For someone workin' in a local jailhouse, that is."

"Thanks for that. Appreciate it."

"Don't mention it. Keep whistlin'."

Travellers

There was a sound of commotion from the front desk. She walked into the salesroom as a flustered assistant rushed past, fleeing four men who stood waiting. Amused. One was stripped to his waste, displaying a gallery of tattoos on beer-swollen flesh.

"Ah, here's the old missus. She'll set us right boys."

Maggie felt mild amusement while giving the group a cool look.

"What's the idea of upsetting my staff then? I've told you before about your manners – and you, what's with the strip show? Are you feeling the heat or is your tiny brain overcooked?"

The man held up his tee-shirt with solemn sobriety, evidence of impeccable intentions.

"Are you not seeing the shirt missus? That's plain writin' there."

On the sweat-soiled shirt was scrawled a line of smudged letters, scruffy graffiti inscribed by a felt-tipped marker pen. She laid the singlet on the counter. It read:

Toomey's Tarmack: Leaves you streeks ahead.

As she considered the lettering, a second figure spoke from a blue shirt, sporting a brown waistcoat that could once have been silk.

"Here's the thing, Missus, and beggin' yer pardon for upsettin' dat wee girl of yours. We're only lookin' to give you a bit of business. Yer see we're needin' ten shirts – no, make it twelve, countin' all the apostles and blessin' holy Saint Peter with the good whisky. We want this writin' on them to show we're the proper thing. Do yet get me, Missus?"

Three fellow apostles nodded in anticipation of glorious deliverance.

"Well, let's see your money and we can talk about turning this rag into something that might look like you've seen the inside of a schoolroom."

"Now, yer not bein' serious with us, are yer, Ma'am? I mean for starters yer never expectin' good money before we've even seen the work are you now? For sure, run a few up and we'll show you the brass, nothin's fairer than that."

She had enough dealings with Irish camp travellers not to be waylaid by their brogue and blandishments. They knew better themselves. No deal was made without money. On the nail.

"I've told you before – it's Eamonn, isn't it?" The spokesman nodded.

"Now isn't that just like yer sweet self, Ma'am? Rememberin' yer best customers and not treating them like common tinkers." He turned to his companions. "Wasn't I tellin' you fellas just that afore we crossed the doorstep? Wasn't I sayin' We'll get the proper job from the Boss Woman and no mistake! Were they not me very words lads?"

The men agreed that Eamonn had expounded such a gospel that very day.

She reiterated, "Twenty quid down."

They looked shocked, as though good faith had been roughly violated. "Sure, Missus, there we were hopin' that twenty would cover the whole job and lettin' you keep the change."

"And I don't know what this scrawl is supposed to mean."

"Now that's easy sorted, Missus. Tell her Seamus."

The man without the shirt was roused from private reverie. "Me writin'? Is it not plain as day, beggin' pardon for yer eyesight, Missus?"

She repeated without flinching, "What does it say?"

Seamus assumed the manner of a kindly bystander helping an infirm person read a road sign, "Well, now, what it's sayin' yer see, is that we fellas are fine craftsmen of the tar – the black muck that is. And we'll do any job – yer driveways, yer footing paths, even patchin' a patio if dat's the job – and leave it like new."

"What is 'Streeks'?"

Here Eamonn returned to the fray. "Ah, dat's the poetry in it, Missus. Michael there." Another comrade raised a hand to claim the name.

"Well, Michael says to us "Yer need a catchy slogan like, for the shirts, so what's about us sayin' something like Streets ahead." Now there's yer real wit, you see. 'Cos we're making the streets black yer see?"

She said nothing. Encouraged, he continued,

"But Seamus gets a shove better. Yer can count on Seamus for makin' up his own words if you're short – gives yer a fine air when the band's playin' or if the brother has a mind to bring out the fiddle. Yer know? So's Seamus says, "No 'Streets', we should put 'Streeks' 'cos dat black stuff's remindin' folk of fast black fellas in them races." That's yer real poet comin' in, yer see Missus?"

"It's streaks with an 'A'. And your tarmac doesn't need a 'K'."

Eamonn was triumphant. "There now, lads! Did I not tell yer that this Missus knew her business, dat she'd set us on a sure road?" To general assent he concluded, "Now, just be tellin' us when they'll be done?"

Maggie could not help feeling a touch of sympathy. They would sweat all day long for a reasonable cash price, making a job that might well look worse after a winter's wear when they would be long gone. Still, the money would fund several nights of determined drinking, sharing the craic.

"I'll do you twelve shirts for £35 and I want £20 down. Be ready by tomorrow morning. What's the colour for the lettering? Tarmac black or blarney green?"

Eamonn considered for a long moment. "Respectin' yer need of the business, Missus, and out of sheer loyalty for yer firm, I'm willin' to break me principles and give twenty down. Its black letters we're wantin' and we're thinkin' that you'll be throwin' in a couple of white shirts to cover the one that Seamus is donatin' here, for yer workers' to get the right idea?"

She slapped a single white tee-shirt on the counter and held out her hand. Eamonn put two tens into it with a smile. "It's grand to see yer makin' such good money out of us poor workin' men and us not begrudgin' it. And all bein' grateful that yer promisin' by the end of the day."

She nodded. "Come back after six. I'll get someone on them this afternoon."

Seamus looked at his new shirt with satisfaction as they departed for some necessary refreshment *en route* back to their camp.

Birthday Suits

It was just possible to hear the voice of Constable Forbes over the static of the walkie talkie radio.] "Hello, Sergeant. Forbes here. We're having some difficulties in Oxford Street."

"Well, Forbes, what is it?"

"We have about forty or fifty demonstrators."

"Is that all? I'd have expected 400 or 500."

"Yes, at least that, Sarg, but we have forty or fifty wearing swimsuits."

"A bit nippy for the sunbathing I think. But no matter, arrest them."

"Are you sure, Sarg?"

"What do you bloody think? The new Covid rules are clear, aren't them, Constable? 'No swimsuits until further notice' or words to that effect. Call in support and get them arrested. They might even welcome getting into a warm police van."

"The thing is, Sarg, they're fully dressed."

"You just said that they're not."

"I said that they're wearing swimsuits. They've got them on top of their clothes. I've got three men in yellow polka dot bikinis and one woman who's wearing some kind of gentlemen's costume – Victorian, I think."

: "Well, we don't make the law and if they have on swimsuits then get them down the station. We can do 'em for disturbing the peace or public disorder if we need to."
: "Right, Sargent. Will do."

The sounds of heckling and disturbance as demonstrators are arrested formed the opening background to the radio news report on the event. *There were scuffles today at the large peaceful demonstration in central London against the recent round of Covid regulations, introduced by the Coalition Government. The Labour Minister of Health said he agreed with the Home Secretary's condemnation of the violence. Pritzi Pangol had stated that people had a right to demonstrate peacefully within the prescribed hours but these individuals had worn swimsuits, clearly designed to provoke confusion and disorder. Sir Michael Bargoe at the Health Department said everyone had a responsibility to protect our NHS from a possible tsunami of Covid infections. Public health meant avoiding crowds and the swimsuit ban had been introduced after three more of the Uganda Variant were traced to an ice-cream hut on Margate Sands. The Minister said the UFO43.B4Z Variant was at least fifteen percent more contagious than the Southend Variant, which had led to the hospitalisation of seventeen people, including a recent traveller from Papua New Guinea on a ventilator. He was suspected of having been infected on a day trip to Hastings, though his condition remained unclear.*

We asked a member of the Scientific Advisory Group for Attitudes (SAGA) for a view on current public opinion. Professor Luke Heckmondlike, chair of their Nerviosa Sub-Committee, told us,

"The country needs to understand just how dangerous the situation could be unless we take control. The Government has said in relation to our recreation, 'Our goal is Desirable Destinations not Day Trips.' The data signals that seaside resorts remain hot spots for spreading this terrible virus. In Eastbourne alone there was a tragic death in a care home of a 94-year-old resident, previously reported as in reasonably good health. It can strike anyone."

As the interview ended, the crowd could be heard singing, All we want for Christmas is a Birthday Suit.'

The television reporter continued,

"We can't show you all of our coverage for obvious reasons but I think you can see enough to indicate that all these people are naked. They're marching down Margate High Street here – you can just see Boots the Chemist and also the Primark store, though I don't suppose they will sell many clothes to this jolly crowd. They are protesting against the banning of swimsuits by the Government. The prohibition on the sale, re-sale, donation or wearing of swimsuits until

October 31 at the earliest is on the roadmap out of the current crisis. These protestors have cast off their swimsuits and are walking to the seafront naked. I spoke to one lady who had just burned her bikini top of a barbecue fire."

Lady demonstrator, "Yes, I'm sixty-eight and I love it. Reminds me of my first husband. We were both naturists you know in Bracken Wood, , near Saint Albans. You're too young to remember but the lady who ran the camp told me that Dr Stephen Ward, the one who fixed up that Profumo politician with Christine Keeler, well, he went to hide there when the scandal broke. Hiding in plain sight you might say."

"So is this an extension of naturism for you? Or is it a political statement?"

"Well, sort of both. I vote Green you know and they're the only party to stand up to this government, aren't they?"

"Would they condone nudist marching – this is a family shopping area?"

"I don't think there's anything to be ashamed of in the human body – we'll all got one. Burning my bikini top just now wasn't any different from burning bras in the sixties – you have to make your point. Sometimes you need a gesture…don't you?"

"That's the view from Margate on a chilly afternoon. Back to you in the warm studio!"

The radio signalled an Official Announcement:

The Cabinet Office has confirmed that the Department of Health guidelines on swimming wear are to be modified to allow the wearing of swimsuits in private gardens where no more than four adults and four children under the age of sixteen are present, including gardens which have private pools or improvised pools in which children may paddle. It is still not permissible for more than four young people aged thirteen to sixteen to congregate in swimwear in public or private places. The department refuses to comment on the current legal action to contest government guidelines which is funded by the Pool Owners' Association and the major swimwear manufacturers. On legal advice the government is seeking to clarify those items of clothing which may be reasonably defined as 'Swimsuits or swimwear'.

Interrupted by a Newsflash: *A Junior Minister has resigned after being photographed jumping into a swimming pool at a birthday party. He was dressed in a dinner jacket and underwear, reported by one witness to be lady's lingerie."*

Fruit Juice (It's a Kind of Fever)

My name is Daniel, Danny, and I'm…well, you know why I'm here. I've been living with this illness for more than three years now. About six months ago I went into some kind of remission. I felt I was getting better, you know? I mean feeling healthy in a way that I had not felt in a long time. My mate Jonno pulled my leg about it when he saw me running, so he shouts, "You're getting your five pieces a day then, hey, Dan?" I could laugh about it by then. My wife hadn't been able to cope with the illness. We broke up about two years ago – but I was got back in touch a while ago and she's in a really good place now. Changed her job and she's coping well. We agreed to share the debts though I wanted to cover them because it was me who couldn't get a job when I was out of it. It wasn't fair on her, all that health crisis stuff she had to go through and no way do I blame her for leaving. She had to look after herself. No point in us all getting ill, is there?

Anyway, I'd been dead careful about my diet and getting enough sleep like they tell us, so it's funny – well, 'ironic' is the word the doctors or therapists would use – that it was the health campaign that set my clock back. There I was doing okay and holding down the job, dealing with the bills now and then one morning I'm walking to work and I see it. Big as three houses put together it was. This massive billboard on the corner near the trading estate. It said, "Have you had your five pieces?" And below the letters were these five pieces of fruit. Like Jonno said. Brilliant colours they were, you know, looking fantastic. Beautiful piece of orange, banana and one that might have been a mango or something exotic. So I stand there and stare at it. There are no plums, I thought, and then my mind was racing, Maybe they're right. Fruit helps the brain. Gets it running.

I carried on to work but all day my mind wasn't on the job. It's on that poster. Right, I thought, I need to take action with this one. Not just let it get to me. So after work I make for the supermarket and I buy as many different kinds of fruit as I can. Not lemons because no one likes lemons, do they? In a gin and tonic maybe but not just as fruit. You can't really like them. They even call dud cars 'lemons', don't they? No one wants them. Pass them on as soon as you can.

When I take my shopping home I sit down and get out the knife and put some of the fruit in a bowl. Couldn't eat them right away so I grilled my beef burger and did some over-ready chips and had my cup of tea. After that I sat there. Staring at the bowl. Finally, I cut an apple in two and I manage to eat that. But it tasted a bit dry, not bitter but dry. Not like the fruit in that poster anyway that apple on up there was as red as Red Riding Hood – or was it Snow White who ate that special apple? Well this apple didn't send me to sleep. It made me feel a bit fidgety. Sometimes fruit does that. If I have an orange at night I can wake up about two in the morning…

Sorry, I'm rambling on here. "Cut to the chase!" and all that. Well, sitting there I could feel the fever hit me. I could feel it coming like a sugar rush. Did my breathing exercises but I was still getting hotter. So I went to the window and tried to calm down. A car passed by – yellow – bright as a banana. Another one. Dark blue. Could be a damson. Then the bus. Lime green with a poster on the side but I pulled my eyes away. It's no good, I thought. I need a drink. Alcohol is just the worst thing, I know because it can lead to a relapse. But I was running out of options. I checked the fridge but I knew there was only fruit juice and that would be a 'return to go', so I get my coat and get to the pub on the corner. Hadn't been there in months. I should have just got the off-licence but I needed a proper pint. Up to the bar, served, and sat down with my drink.

I knew he was there waiting for me over in the corner. My old mate and just the worst friend in the world. As soon as I heard him, I knew there was no avoiding it. I had to have a word. Resisted as long as I could. Even told myself I was going to the toilet but I stopped and turned to him. He was, what would you say, 'magnetic'. So I sat and as soon as I pulled his arm I knew I was there for the night. Up it came, right as rain. Two lemons and an orange. No plums. I spent everything I had, about forty quid and even won ten back at one point. But there was only one way that could end. With my pockets empty. Just like the old days. I thought to myself, This is my life. Fruit machines are my life.

I could have gone on a bender and I didn't. Not yet. So I came here and tell you about it. It's a relapse. No question. Well, that's me. My name is Danny and I'm a gambling addict. Thank you.

Fig Leaves

They had finally decided to let Dunstan come home. Gervase sat watching the reflection of the afternoon sunshine on the green water of the old swimming pool, built before the war with a benefaction from one of the school's wealthy pupils. The bench on which he sat was at the far end of a derelict orchard, surrounded by a scent of wild garlic. The only fruit which fell in this place now were memories of much earlier years when this abbey claimed a full complement of monks, many of them young men with a zest for sports as much as spiritual exercises. Numbers had dwindled after the excitement of the 1960s passed and now they were barely sufficient to meet all the obligations of the great monastery and its sprawling school premises.

Among the younger monks enjoying that dawn of optimism in the Church, Dunstan was unquestionably the most brilliant. The most original thinker of his novitiate with an intellect that flourished in visits to Rome and Germany. Gervase recalled how his radical ideas for reform had appalled older conservative monks, raised in the long traditions of the Latin Church and lurid accounts of monastic martyrdom in Protestant countries. Unreliable as a teacher who could coach slower boys towards the examination success that their parents paid for and expected, Dunstan had a passionate following among the brighter pupils who would congregate in his rooms listening to Sibelius until midnight. Personally beautiful, he attracted the boys who shared his glamorous gifts and his stamina for long expeditions across the surrounding countryside.

It was easy to fall in love with Dunstan's personality. Gervase had loved him from the early days of their novitiate with a sober love that understood his brilliant colleague's flaws as well as undeniable charm. Everything was of the moment for Dunstan. In the time you spent with him, you enjoyed his undivided attention and his boundless enthusiasm for everything fresh. Naturally musical, he would carry groups to the organ and bang out a Latin hymn with the energy of a pop group. Once the moment of magic had passed, he was moving to other things, happily unconscious of those left behind. He excelled in attachments but they never constrained him from fresh ventures and here lay the root of the scandal that abruptly miscarried his brilliant career as a monk.

Among the boys, young Neville was one of his most ardent admirers, hanging on such exciting words as 'transcendental' which came so easily to his teacher. While the other boys could be enthralled by Dunstan's personality, Neville felt an utter devotion to him that his idol understood but didn't encourage. Neville could be included in some ventures and excluded from others. For Dunstan was blithely unaware of the pain caused by casual neglect of his devotees. The clouds gathered over their relationship and Neville began to avoid his master. Gervase had seen the difficulty and encouraged the pupil to spend more time with the other boys. Then it happened. As Dunstan emerged from Vespers early one evening, Neville appeared and without hesitation kissed Dunstan in view of some older monks. Dunstan eased himself away and simply smiled saying, "It's good you are back in the fray Neville. Your last essay was really quite good." With this he turned and walked away, leaving the boy who seemed somehow triumphant.

Inevitably there was a serious outcome from this unexpected encounter if only because some older monks strongly resented Dunstan's apparent indifference to their values, which they mistook as irreverence for sacred tradition. No one could have expected matters to escalate with such speed. The Prior called me to provide an account of the incident. Then the Abbot interviewed Dunstan and within a week it was announced that he would be leaving the monastic community, at least for a period. When I spoke to him, he was oddly stoical about his departure. "Neville told the Abbot that it was common for us to kiss and that I had initiated the whole thing in my rooms one night. So the Abbot decided I had to go."

"But, Dunstan, was it true?"

"Of course not. I've never kissed the boy. But I have been thinking for quite a while that it was time for me to widen my horizons. This place doesn't expand the mind, does it?"

Dunstan left the abbey the following week and within a month he was declared *ex claustra*, excluded from the community. Some of us raised a protest with the Abbot but were told that this had been agreed with Dunstan himself. He never returned. Within a year or two he had left the monastic life and became a successful teaching and writer, publishing significant books on the place of desire in the spiritual life. Neville avoided contact with other boys and monks, becoming a solitary figure, elusive and self-absorbed. Gervase found him sitting in the disused cricket pavilion one afternoon and he saw that some explanation was unavoidable. He frowned a little and said with a clear face, "It's that fig story from Mark's gospel, Father Gervase."

"Go on."

"Well, Jesus should have known that it wasn't the season for figs but he saw the tree in leaf so he went to look for a fig and didn't find one. He cursed the tree."

"Meaning what, Neville?"

"Father Dunstan should have known that we can't always give him the fruit he desired. It's the curse of Christ. "Can people pick grapes from thorns or figs from thistles?" Despise us and we wither. My thorn was that kiss of betrayal."

Pausing, I asked if he wanted to tell the Abbot the truth about the kiss. He simply shook his head. "It's best this way" is all he would say.

In one of his last letters Dunstan told me that he had asked to be laid to rest back here. "Don't be surprised," he wrote, "I've always been a bit of a closet conservative."